SNAPSHOTS

SNAPSHOTS

A Collection of Short Stories

ELIOT PARKER

NEW YORK

LONDON • NASHVILLE • MELBOURNE • VANCOUVER

Snapshots

A Collection of Short Stories

Published in New York, New York, by Morgan James Publishing. Morgan James is a trademark of Morgan James, LLC. www.MorganJamesPublishing.com

ISBN 9781642797138 paperback
ISBN 9781642797145 eBook
Library of Congress Control Number: 2019947247

Cover Design by:
Megan Dillon
megan@creativeninjadesigns.com

Interior Design by:
Chris Treccani
www.3dogcreative.net

Morgan James is a proud partner of Habitat for Humanity Peninsula and Greater Williamsburg. Partners in building since 2006.

Get involved today! Visit
MorganJamesPublishing.com/giving-back

Also by
ELIOT PARKER

Breakdown at Clear River
Making Arrangements

Ronan McCullough Novels
Fragile Brilliance
A Knife's Edge

Stacy Tavitt Novels
Code for Murder

SOME STORIES IN THE COLLECTION
WERE PREVIOUSLY PUBLISHED:

"Hands." *Speck* Literary Journal 2011.

"Reflections." *Flash: An Anthology*
(KY Story Publications), February 2012.

"Reckless." *Appalachian Undead*
(Apex Books), October 2012.

"Hub 2000." Crack The Spine Literary Anthology,
November 2013.

"Snapshots." *Diner Stories*
(Mountain State Press), January 2015.

*A good snapshot stops a
moment from going away.*

Eudora Welty

Hands

With fingertips soaked in blood, Conley adjusted the wide-brimmed, transparent helmet covering his face then lifted a fold of dense muscle near the ribcage and began threading the flesh with heavy twine. As he started the balletic weaving of string through the terse tissue, seamlessly sewing up the patient, Conley leaned closer.

The metal operating table felt cold on Conley's forearms as he repositioned himself, hovering mere inches away from the body. He made a final incision with the needle then tugged on the twine and wove it directly around the nipple.

Rising slowly, he let out a long, exasperated breath, and the warm air trapped inside the mask clouded his eyesight. Conley turned away from the body and approached the surgical sink where he slouched and lowered his hands under the motion-activated nozzle as a generous stream of warm water trickled from the spigot. As the blood on his plastic-coated fingers mixed with the water, it dissipated. He disposed of the latex gloves as the mask vapor faded, then he washed his hands and removed the mask.

Conley narrowed his eyes as he located a file folder near the burgundy sink ledge adjacent to the operating table. Picking up the folder, he scribbled notes on the parchment document.

The swinging morgue doors thrust open, and a burst of warm air rushed into the room. A large shadow approached Conley. He turned and his face tightened.

Conley stopped writing. Lowering the folder and dropping the pen on the sink table, he squinted, studying the approaching figure closely.

A halogen lamp, which arched overhead and separated Conley and the stationary body from the oncoming shadow, cast enough illumination to define the figure's features.

With fair hair, a sharp chin, and blue eyes, the pale, clean-shaven man sauntered past the stainless-steel operating table. The lethargic gait of the man made him appear a schlub. Dressed in a banal blue suit, paired with a white shirt and purple tie, the man leaned his slight frame against the sink counter and ran a set of fingers through his hair.

"She's beautiful."

"And dead," Conley added dryly. He lowered his gaze and felt Bill slowly watching his movements.

As Conley stood over the deceased woman lying before them, her body stoically calm, a chill went through Conley. A quick roll of his shoulders shook away the feeling as he reached for and ensnared the pen from the sink counter, momentarily locking gazes with Bill again.

Removing his focus from Conley, Bill unbuttoned the suit jacket and traced the woman's hands with two of his own slender fingers. As he retraced the outline, he did not look up but mumbled a question for clarification.

"So, she did okay?"

"Just okay," Conley responded. "She bled quite a bit, and she had some internal organ trauma, but once the machine latched onto the blood vessel, everything calmed down."

Bill nodded. "Good. We need to make sure she is ready for tomorrow."

From the corner of his eye, Conley watched Bill open a cabinet drawer with a practiced movement. Bill removed a small, stout glass jar from the cabinet along with a fluffy, flat pad. At the same time, Conley frantically scribbled information onto the paper inside the folder.

As Conley continued writing, Bill unscrewed the cap and slapped powdery, white chalk on his hands, then walked around the base of the table and stood over the woman. "You can finish her face," Bill demanded, his voice full and authoritative as he patted the woman's hands with the pad covered in chalk.

Conley peered over the top of the file folder and chuckled.

"What's so funny?" Bill asked.

Conley appreciated the strange, unassuming demeanor Bill normally displayed. When Bill was flustered, Conley took great joy in watching him not rush his words but pronounce each syllable deliberately.

"You never look at the people on the table," Conley said, lifting a foot and resting it against the sink counter. "As many years as you've been doing this, you would think your phobia would subside." Conley wrote the name *Julia Thomas* on the blank file folder tab.

"It's not a phobia," Bill replied defensively. "I just don't want to be the last person to look into the eyes of the deceased."

"I still think it's a bit ridiculous." Conley closed the folder and set it aside then looked at Bill, who gave a few more delicate strokes of the pad with frown lines creasing his brow.

Conley looked at Julia's inert form. She was indeed beautiful. Her face was square with unblemished skin. She had thick, full lips that were pursed outward and a taut, curvy physique that made her appear much younger. Her eyes were light blue and buoyant at the corners, revealing a fragile, congenial innocence. The woman appeared angelic, situated comfortably on the table.

Bill cleared his throat. "I hope this powder is enough. She had such beautiful hands. Sometimes, restoring them to their natural state is hard no matter how much powder is used."

As Conley walked around the table, the mint-green lab jacket he wore billowed outward and grazed Bill. The motion startled Bill, and he nearly stumbled. Regaining his balance, he stood upright with his chest extended and his hands unclenched.

"You made the removal, Bill. Why don't you go home and get some sleep? The family wants the body taken to the cemetery for a sunrise service in the morning. I can finish up here."

Bill let the words settle. "The only thing left to do is powder her face."

Conley collected another jar and pad. Turning sharply, Conley studied Bill, watching carefully as his whole countenance softened.

"I just don't want to look at her while I am doing it," Bill said, the words echoing throughout the room.

"I've changed my mind," Conley responded sprightly. "Your phobia is totally ridiculous."

"I don't think so," Bill said.

"Why do you feel the way you do about the deceased and their eyes, anyway?"

"I have been doing this a long time," Bill said. He looked up and past Conley, who was tenderly padding the woman's face.

"My family has been in this business for seventy years. My grandfather told my dad, who told me, that if you look into the eyes of the deceased, your soul will be taken to purgatory."

When Conley waved away the comment and laughed aloud, Bill made a face.

"It sounds like an old urban legend or a nonsensical piece of folklore to me," Conley said. "Did your grandfather or your father experience what you're telling me?"

Bill lowered his chin and spoke softly, "Well, no."

"See what I mean? Your grandfather and father were just scaring you. Every profession has superstitions and old wives' tales. They were just passing this one on to the next generation and using it to scare you a bit."

Bill stepped back from the hovering light. A shadow divided his face at the bridge of the nose.

Conley heard Bill breathing more shallowly.

"I will prove your superstition is nonsense. Watch what I'm doing."

Putting the pad and powder back on the table, Conley leaned forward and stared intently into the eyes of the woman. Her light blue eyes were flat yet still full of color, and they remained motionless. Conley heard Bill yelp slightly under his breath.

Conley held the look for a few long moments and then stood up, extended his arms, and spun around.

"See, I did it, and I am still here." Conley observed Bill standing firmly and stiffly in front of him, almost as rigidly and firmly as the woman residing on the table.

A strangled smile finally crept across Bill's face. "Well, don't say I didn't warn you." Waving a disapproving finger at Conley, Bill backpedaled and left the morgue.

After another hour of cosmetology and a trip to the morgue basement, the body and casket of Julia Thomas were ready for burial.

Conley wheeled the casket onto the morgue elevator. After turning a switch, the elevator swayed from side to side as the machine motor ground, lowering the elevator car slowly.

Conley removed a small pocket mirror. Wearing tapered trousers and a solid white, button-up shirt tucked in at the waist with the shirt collar undone, he felt beads of sweat streaking down his back. Looking at the face in the mirror, he grimaced disapprovingly at his reflection in the glass.

Conley concentrated on his boyish features, including his ears, which protruded from closely cropped auburn hair that disguised a small round face. Tiny freckles splotched across his forehead and cheeks, and they seemed to multiply the longer he stared into the mirror.

Shivering despairingly, he tucked the mirror back inside his pocket.

Using a mechanical lift in the garage, Conley loaded the body of Julia Thomas inside the hearse. He felt stately and regal sitting inside the hearse. Its fully painted roof, along with recessed crown molding and landau bars, gave the car a class and elegance fit for the deceased's last ride of luxury.

Conley got in the hearse, started the engine, and drove the car out of the garage. The night sky featured descending moonlight and the slowly emerging sun that fractured the hazy, humid air, turning the clouds into a kaleidoscope of color with dark red and fiery orange streaks of light making a temporary imprint above. Conley felt calm and resolute he tapped the accelerator pedal.

As he approached the cemetery outside of town, an ornamental iron fence, which seemed out of place, greeted Conley, along with graves scattered throughout the overgrown and unkempt grounds.

Conley pulled the hearse away from the narrow, paved road. Seven erect tombs on the western side of the cemetery grounds, harboring inscriptions on the doors, stood open, the entryways covered with debris.

He loved the traditional family cemetery. This small space had an aura of hallowed ground. Conley removed the casket from the hearse, placed it on a large silver gurney, and wheeled it inside one of the dark, empty tombs. He kept his eyes closed throughout the process, ensuring the sanctity and privacy of others would be respected.

Proceeding back to the hearse, Conley felt the early morning humidity hang in the sky like a thick wool blanket, and with its suffocating persistence, the air felt heavy in the lungs, forcing him to breath heavily. Conley observed many broken gravestones speckled with a granular substance, which made them difficult to interpret or read.

From a distance, Conley noticed a woman approaching. Intrigued and curious, his eyes narrowed on the woman. With low-hanging bangs, flowing red hair, and black glasses, the woman stared at Conley with an expression both wary and challenging. Dressed in jeans and sneakers and clad in a blue windbreaker, the woman appeared underdressed for the occasion and overdressed for the weather.

"You scared me," she shouted in a full-throated tone tinged with anger.

Conley cupped his hands around his mouth and replied, "Likewise."

The rising sunlight cast a faint orange glow around the woman, so Conley shielded the light from his eyes by placing an open hand over his right eye, but the sun crept in through the space between his fingers. He wiped his damp forehead with his left hand.

He went to speak, but no words emerged. Conley finally positioned his right hand in a position away from his face, which visually settled the woman's appearance within his sun-splashed eyes.

The innocent face of the woman, fine-boned and striking with penetrating slate gray eyes and a dissatisfied lower lip, distorted into a scowl.

"I'm sorry. I didn't mean to scare you. I am wondering what you're doing."

"My name is Conley Ward, and I'm from Manning Funeral Home. Are you here to see Miss Thomas?" Conley flashed a compassionate grin.

The woman pressed her lips tightly together and reached down to scratch her leg.

Conley stood motionless, and she placed her hands on her hips.

"Honestly, I am trying to figure out why my friend is an hour late for our appointment."

Staring intently at her pursed lips and voluptuous figure as she spoke, Conley felt an odd sense of familiarity with the woman, the type that comes from meeting someone once and then being reacquainted with them sometime later.

Conley felt his cheeks sting as he responded, "Well, these days, canceling appointments should be easy. I sometimes think because we have so many ways to keep in touch with people, we're worse at doing it if that makes any sense."

His stomach fluttered. Conley wondered if the last statement made any sense at all.

The woman turned around and glanced at the small, sprawling cemetery as a light burst of wind tossed her thick, curly sandy hair behind her shoulders. When she turned back around to face Conley again, her gaze studied him closely.

Conley leaned forward slightly, hiding the rising sunlight from his face.

The woman bit her lower lip and spoke sweetly, "Why don't you come around and get out of the sun?"

She flashed a toothy, seductive grin, and Conley's chest swelled with excitement and anxiety. Conley noticed a smell radiating from her that was cloying in its sweetness.

"I'm Jessica!" the woman said sprightly, flashing another wide smile at Conley.

Conley nodded, surprised by her overt introduction, which stood in stark contrast to the way he was feeling. He dropped his chin and observed a thin hand with five fingers pressing lightly against his sternum, feeling small pools of perspiration form as Jessica touched him.

Uncertain about the awkward gesture, he raised his right hand and interlocked his pudgy fingers around Jessica's slender fingers. She displayed a surprisingly firm grip, although her hands were quite cold and clammy for such a sultry morning.

Jessica momentarily winced and stared at him intently. At first, Conley maintained a strong grip, but with the aid of her left hand, Jessica pried open their interlocked grip and began stroking the palm of his hand with her fingertips.

"I spend a lot of time at this cemetery," she said softly. "I have lost so many friends and family members over the years, and many of them are buried here. But I have gained so many friends as well."

Conley furrowed his brow and leveled another look at Jessica. He was unsure of her age, and although she appeared youthful, Conley could not part with the feeling of having met the woman before.

His rough and calloused hands shook as she stroked them, and the gesture made Conley shiver. A woman he knew nothing about, performing such a tender gesture, made Conley sway from side to side.

Jessica, noticing the motion dropped her gaze, but she did not move. Lightly stroking the palm of his hand, her gaze locked with Conley's once again. "Your hands…they are so flat and rough," Jessica said.

Conley laughed nervously. "I make my living from my hands. I'm afraid, in the process, I have not taken very good care of them."

Intrigued, Jessica curled her lips inward. "And what is it that you do exactly, Conley?"

He pulled his left hand away from Jessica's grasp and waived it indiscriminately at her.

"I work with people on a daily basis, and my hands help me do that," he said, finally speaking with an authoritative thunder in his voice. "My hands help me comfort and take care of people and their families during a sorrowful moment in their lives." Conley closed his lips and swallowed a large gulp of air before he continued, "My job requires a principled sense of responsibility along with warmth and compassion. I have to be skilled with my hands as well as my heart. I think I make a difference for many people dealing with grief. The emotional toll can sometimes be exasperating."

"Interesting," she remarked with a faint touch of curiosity in her voice.

Another sudden gust of warm air blew between them. Conley noticed a faint twinkle in the woman's eyes.

"I wish I could help other people," she added. "I mean like you do. It sounds to me like you make a big difference in the lives of others."

"I get a chance to really know people personally as well as learn their family history." Conley paused thoughtfully and then chuckled. "Sometimes, you learn the dynamics of the family, but when you learn about the individual and how the individual relates to his or her family, then you can help everyone."

Jessica stepped back and crossed her arms. "You do this every day of your life? Do the demands of dealing with these people every day bother you?"

"Honestly, it can be exhausting but rewarding," Conley replied confidently. "When you see that you have helped the family with your hands and your heart, even the experiences of working with a challenging or awkward family leave you with a good feeling." He felt satisfied in his response.

Jessica ran her light pink tongue across her thin lips. Smacking them together, she tucked a tuft of hair behind her right ear.

Unsure why she was interested in his work life, Conley shifted the focus of the conversation back to her.

"So, what is it that you do?"

Confidently, Jessica leaned forward. "Nothing...at...all." She carefully enunciated each syllable in the phrase, the words piercing the air.

Conley scoffed, "Great. But really, what do you do?"

She tilted her head to the left and scowled, a bit offended that he didn't believe her.

Conley watched her face soften and almost exhaled a sense of relief. He studied her smooth and delicate cheeks, full of the most magnificent peach hue. Fascinated by her physically, Conley could not move, although his stiff muscles sent tremors of pain throughout his body.

As Jessica leaned forward, her warm breath careening near his nose, Conley also leaned closer, almost hypnotically. He should be watching the crypt and Julia Thomas as he waited for her family to arrive.

Jessica blushed and cleared her throat. "I expand my circle of friends, especially male friends. Guys are so much easier to talk to and be with…" Her voice descended and then trailed off entirely.

Her shoulders bobbed and weaved as she leaned closer toward him.

With the tips of their noses touching, she parted her lips slightly, and Conley felt her warmth protruding from her mouth. She placed a soft kiss on his lips.

Momentarily paralyzed, Conley attempted to speak but couldn't breathe much less talk.

Jessica lightly touched his face. "Let me show you something," she said pleadingly, encouraging Conley to follow.

Breathless and speechless, Conley felt his head pounding and his heartbeat racing faster and faster. His mouth was as dry as a charred forest. Conley blinked. As he followed her, she appeared to glide over the cemetery grounds, her blue windbreaker billowing as she moved.

As Conley looked behind him to ensure the stability and safety of the hearse, he heard another vehicle come to a screeching stop. Julia's parents emerged from a red car, giving no indication that they saw Conley or Jessica.

Jessica led Conley over a few slight hills towards the back of the cemetery. The faint orange light created by the early morning sunlight disappeared, and cold wind wisped at their feet. Jessica turned her head, smiled seductively at Conley, and then walked faster.

Near the last hill of the cemetery, a freshly dug grave, slightly covered with clumps of grass and twigs, rested below a shining pewter gravestone.

She stopped walking and turned to face Conley.

Conley watched intently as her face paled and her eyes turned almost black. Jessica leaned in, and her face suddenly appeared composed entirely of muscle and jawbone.

Conley felt his heart sink.

For a moment, Conley closed his eyes but then reopened them. He heard Bill calling his name in the distance, but Conley could not respond.

When Jessica stepped away, the name *Conley Ward* was chiseled into the face of the gravestone in front of him. Conley wiped his damp fingers on his charcoal-gray dress pants.

She grabbed him by the hands again. "Come with me. Come with me. Come with me."

Conley watched as Jessica took a short breath, held it, and then exhaled. A small stream of opaque dust discharged from her nose and mouth, and she blew the milky, odorless cloud at Conley. The dust made his nose tingle, and he suddenly found it difficult to breathe.

"Come with me, Conley." The more Jessica recited those words, the more cryptic they seemed.

Conley dug the heels of his dress shoes into the freshly turned earth, but instead of slowing his momentum, the move pushed him closer.

Jessica laughed seductively. The fresh dirt and debris covering the grave faded away, and she stepped inside it.

Conley, hearing Bill approaching quickly, attempted to scream, hoping that Bill would hear him. Conley couldn't move nor stop the progression into the hole.

When Jessica tightened her grip and dug her nails into his flesh, his parched mouth was pried opened in pain. She covered it tightly with her other hand. Her hand smelled like death and paralyzed his ability to scream.

Conley managed a question, and although it seemed to him he spoke loudly, the words escaped like a whisper.

"Where are you taking me?"

Jessica licked her lips again. "To hell."

Hub2000

I looked at my work schedule for the last time, and as my downcast eyes looked away, I crumpled the paper in my hand and rested my cheek against the window. The bus had been driving through the serpentine swaths of the two-lane airport road for the last thirty minutes. In the distance, I heard the thrust reduction sounds of airplanes growing louder as we approached the warehouse.

As the bus veered to the left and began slowing, I bent my knees slightly to absorb the motion. When the bus stopped at the last pickup point, I looked straight ahead, silently counting down the seconds. This was my last five-minute midnight stop at the Hub2000 employee terminal. After four years of working the graveyard shift for United Parcel Service, I was moving away from Louisville with a business degree and the hopes of a career.

Several employees filed out of the last terminal, an elongated building with soaring glass walls and a flowing roofline. The driver lurched forward and pulled back on the lever, opening the doors. Most of the men quietly boarded and plopped down in a seat close to the front of the bus. They were smart because the closer you were to the front of the bus, the smoother the ride to the warehouse, but I liked the anonymity and silence that came from sitting in the rear of the vehicle.

The bus doors had nearly closed when someone close to the driver yelped. The driver bounced upright slightly in his chair and sighed then swung the lever again, reopening the doors as another worker stumbled up the steps.

Once he collected himself, the lithe figure at the front of the bus leaned into the driver and spoke. The driver dismissed him with the wave of a hand and released the parking brake.

His shadow came into focus as he scoured the bus. Some men leaned against the window while others talked quietly to one another, but nobody seemed interested in relinquishing any seating space. The bus began moving forward, and he grabbed the back of an empty seat. By standing diagonally in the bus, he achieved the lateral stability he needed to walk forward. Still, standing on this bus was like trying to skateboard.

His gaze locked with mine, and he did not relinquish the stare as he grinned and kept approaching. I closed my eyes for a moment, and when I reopened them, he sat down on the seat in front of me.

Before I could take a deep breath of relief, he turned sideways. "I'm Bryce Byrnes. This is my first day."

I blinked. "I'm Owen. Owen Halloway. You have all the rookie excitement. I remember those days."

The corners of his mouth drew up into a smile. "This job is going to be great. I can get my tuition paid for at Jefferson CTC and still take classes during the day. I'm stoked!"

I'd felt the same way when I signed on to work for UPS at the Worldport. Its name was the Hub2000 after UPS spent millions of dollars in 2000 at Louisville International Airport, building new warehouses and constructing new runways for their planes. Many of the jobs at the Hub2000 were part-time and overnight, which were attractive prospects for college students.

When I was fretting about how I was going to be able to go to school at the University of Louisville and find a job that would help pay the bills, a financial aid counselor recommended talking to a recruiter with UPS. I made my way to the career fair and met with the recruiter. At first, the burly man with short, cropped hair and dark eyes intimidated me. Those eyes seemed fixed in an intense expression. He told me UPS offered a tuition reimbursement program where students who worked part-time overnight could receive one hundred percent tuition reimbursement and earn a ten-dollars-an-hour wage. When I accepted the job, I was surprised to learn on my first day that most of the workers at the Hub2000 were students.

Bryce rubbed both hands together. He was a sophisticated boy with high planed cheeks, wide eyes, and curly light-brown hair.

"Did you know that the Hub is the size of eighty football fields and is capable of handling eighty-four packages a second or four hundred and sixteen thousand per hour?"

I cocked my head sideways and let it nudge the glass window again. "No, I didn't, but thanks for that information."

Bryce laid his palms flat and pushed himself up from the seat until he rested on his knees, and leaned closer. "I hope we can work together."

Feigning a smile, I said, "We probably won't be working together. This is my last night working at the Hub."

Bryce chewed on the inside of his cheek, letting the statement resonate for a moment. "Then maybe you can introduce me to some people. I'm from Hodgenville, and I don't know anybody in Louisville. Shoot, I've never done anything that paid ten dollars an hour!"

Before I could respond, Bryce continued.

"What's it like working here? Is it fun? Do we stay busy? Is your boss nice?" His animated face dimmed a bit when a shadow washed over the bus as we passed through the runway lights and those from the southern passenger terminal of the airport.

The bus jerked to a stop, and I nodded at Bryce. "You'll learn more tonight." As I leaned away from the window, I was a bit surprised that my shoulders had gone to sleep. I rolled them, trying to get that sensation of needles floating in my skin to go away.

Bryce got up and looked down, running his hands over the uniform to smooth out the wrinkles. He wore the standard-issue, chocolate brown attire, and the button-down shirt hugged him tightly. However, he was wearing shorts, although he got the socks right. They allowed us to wear shorts instead of pants, but we had to purchase UPS-approved brown socks.

I let out a soft laugh as we moved to the front of the bus. "Your knees are going to get skinned up wearing shorts. The steel floors of those Boeing 757s are pretty unforgiving."

He turned back to me for a moment and furrowed his brow. "We will be working on our hands and knees?"

I nodded again. "Yep. A lot."

Once off the bus, I stepped past Bryce and began walking to the warehouse, but I heard him taking long strides behind me, trying to catch up. A few hundred yards away from the warehouse, I saw a UPS 757 shoot down a runway, and the plane emanated a loud, growling noise. I'd learned the growl meant the pilots were not performing a full-thrust takeoff, which usually meant the aircraft was not full of cargo.

The one-story, brown-brick warehouse had three corrugated metal airplane hangar doors that were open. Another door near the end of the warehouse, this one made of thick steel, was closed. There were no windows in front, and not a single sign to identify who or what might be inside.

As the group approached the doors, the silhouette of a Boeing 757 became more defined as the overhead lights bathed the inside hangar in soft white light. The light accentuated the two turbofan engines, tail, and supercritical wing designs, which gave the wings a flattened upper surface. The plane appeared stately in its stoic condition, although the rear hatch doors were open and the platform ramp had already been nestled against the butt of the plane.

I turned away from the aircraft and headed to the time clock room to punch in and begin my shift. Before I got close, Bryce grabbed my arm.

I groaned, and he walked around me. "Is this it? Is this our hangar?" He stepped back and craned his neck up, examining the plane with wide-eyed optimism. "Amazing! What do we do? I know. I bet we need to climb up the ramp and start unloading."

Bryce ran to the ramp, and I grabbed the arm of a colleague passing by whose bright blue eyes fixed on me with a wistful expression.

"Go get Mike. Tell him we have a rookie."

He walked faster toward the time clock room, hollering Mike's name. I ran behind Bryce, who was now standing halfway up the platform ramp.

"What are you doing?" I asked in frustration.

He ignored me, and I watched as he touched his index finger to his forehead in spontaneous meditation. "I bet we move the heavy packages out first. They are the heaviest and will take the most time to move." He snapped his fingers. "Right."

Mike's booming voice arose behind me. "Stop! Get down from there!"

I felt Mike's warm breath on my neck through his heavy pants and heaves. Bryce froze, and then he slowly backpedaled down the ramp and turned around.

Mike walked around me. He was a big, easy fellow with a trim goatee and a slightly southern drawl, but he was nobody's fool, especially for an overzealous rookie employee he'd never met.

Bryce extended both arms outward, and Mike stopped. "I'm sorry. I didn't mean to upset you. I'm Bryce. I'm new, and I'm ready to go."

I saw Mike's shoulders bounce and saw him shift his weight. "We have procedures and policies around here, son. They exist for a reason. Everyone knows them, and everyone follows them." He looked past Bryce and pointed to the inside of the plane. "If you had injured yourself up there without the proper forms being filled out, OSHA would shut us down in a minute." The veins in Mike's neck bulged, and his cheeks filled with blood. He looked Bryce over. "Besides, you might be too frail for this job anyway." Some of the other guys gathering around us overheard and laughed. I patted my stomach and considered this. It was one of those rare times I was thankful for my husky build.

Bryce rested his hands on his narrow hips and stuck out his chest. "I just wanted to help; that's all. I know trying to move four hundred and sixteen thousand packages an hour means there's no time to waste—"

"Cut the crap, will ya?" Mike interjected. He dropped his chin and shook his head. "I know the corporate garbage they put in the brochures about this place."

"I-I just…" Bryce's stammering made some of the guys laugh harder.

"You need to know a few things, son. First, we do preload. You know what that is?" Bryce arched an eyebrow but remained silent. "In preload, all the packages from the plane are mapped based on the route schedule, keeping in mind priority deliveries and bulk items. Then we do a morning stretch for fifteen minutes. I don't want any of my workers injuring themselves unloading packages from this plane. Then we have a meeting to discuss general business, safety, and any new regulations. Then, and only then, do we begin unloading packages."

Mike cut a sharp look at me and lowered his voice to a low rumble. "Is he a friend of yours, Halloway?"

I shook my head. "No, sir. I just met him earlier tonight on the bus."

"Good," Mike replied. He reached a meaty hand behind me and slapped my back. "You are going to be his mentor. Show him the ropes."

"But, Mike, it's my last night—"

"Doesn't matter," he said, shielding the light over his eyes with one hand and squinting. "You're one of my best workers. He can learn a lot from you tonight. Besides, it looks like we've got a light plane to unload anyway."

From the corner of my eye, I saw Bryce looking down at the stained concrete floor, tapping his foot in a nonsensical pattern and whistling quietly.

"Byrnes!" Mike said in a voice that was smaller but tenser.

Bryce froze and slowly met Mike's gaze.

"Procedures." Mike hesitated before speaking again. "We have procedures, which I am going to explain to you but only once. Then I expect you to follow them."

Bryce bobbled his head in agreement.

Mike looked at me again, this time a bit longer than before. "Watch him carefully," he said with his voice a near whisper.

"I will," I replied.

Mike motioned for Bryce to follow him, and immediately the crew and I assumed our usual workstations throughout the hangar.

Most of my coworkers ran to the left quadrant of the hangar and turned on the conveyor belts. In a few minutes, the belts would rise and fall as packages of all sizes whizzed by in multiple directions.

I climbed the ramp with George, a compact sophomore at the University of Louisville with shaggy black hair, squared glasses, and arched eyebrows. The pungent smell of jet fuel still wafted through the plane, making my eyes water. The two under floor cargo holds of the plane seemed deep and cavernous, although the open lower deck doors, when closed, divided the smaller space in the forward compartment from the deeper space in the aft one. We pulled the packages off and slid them down the ramp.

A few guys at the bottom collected then walked the packages over to the first conveyor belt. For a while, it would travel from one belt to another before they were eventually loaded onto another dock. Then the package would be taken from the dock and put on a truck that would take it to its final destination.

A lanky shadow approached. I saw George look up then away.

"I don't think I've signed my name so many times in my life," Bryce said. "Mike didn't have to be such a grouch, either."

I kept unloading the packages, now fully comfortable in the hypnotic rhythm of sliding packages behind me. I hoped Bryce would be quiet and just observe what we were doing.

He grabbed a small box from George and lifted it up, swiveled it in his hands, and inspected it.

I peered at him, making sure he wasn't going to drop the package, while George silently reached around him and pulled another package toward the ramp.

A look of concern crossed Bryce's face. He lowered the box and held it tightly against his body.

"What happens if we make a mistake?" Bryce asked.

George cleared his throat and glared at me over the top of his glasses. "You want me to take this one, or do you want it?"

The muscles in my throat tightened. I just wanted to get through the night quietly. Bryce pursed his lips, waiting for an answer.

"When we take a package from the plane, the first conveyor belt takes it with the label facing up and to the left. We have five scanners that scan the label and then use the information from the label to direct the package onto the next belt, which will get it closer to the right dock." I leaned back against the wall of the plane, the cool steel comforting my sweat-splotched back.

Bryce nodded slowly, tightened the muscles in his face, and stared down at the package he was holding.

"But, Owen, the packages move from belt to belt without stopping."

"True. That's the beauty of the system. That's how we are able to move four hundred and sixteen thousand packages a night." I grinned sheepishly at Bryce and went back to work.

"Let me have that one," George commanded, reaching out and taking the box from Bryce. In one smooth motion, George snatched the box and slid it down the ramp.

"Go ahead and start grabbing the boxes and sliding them to George and me," I told Bryce, who crouched down and hesitated. "It doesn't matter what size or shape you pull first. Just get them off the plane."

We pulled packages and shoved them down the ramp for a while. Mike walked past our operation several times, folding his arms, and observing our work. When he passed by the second time, Bryce stopped moving.

"This one is leaking," he said, his voice slightly tinged with panic.

A glance passed between George and me, and we kept working.

"Guys, I'm serious," Bryce pleaded, dropping the package between us. The box listed to one side then fell back on its four corners.

I slid back against the curved metal of the cargo hold, not wanting to touch the box as a thick, black liquid oozed from the corner of the box and pooled on the floor.

George crept closer to the liquid and sniffed. Bryce gasped. "It doesn't smell like anything," George said. "I'll get Mike."

After a few moments of confusion, Mike marched over to us and moved the package, wearing his protective gloves and a mask. The liquid was slick and trickled through his fingers. A scan of the label indicated the package was from Milton Freeman and addressed to Dustin Pike with a destination in Saginaw, Michigan. Inside the package was supposed to be a remote-controlled airplane.

"I'm going to call the airport police and fire rescue just to make sure this is nothing serious," Mike said. "In the meantime, you need to take this package outside and away from the building."

I was standing outside the group of guys that encircled Mike, and I did not observe who was involved with the directive. The whispered tangents of the other guys caught my attention.

"Halloway, you and Byrnes take this thing out back and set it in that open space between the hangars."

I looked at Mike with his thoughtful, hooded eyes while Bryce looked at me with his customary facial expression—a faint smile with the middle-distance squint of someone lost in abstraction.

"Now!" Mike barked. "We've got work to do and deadlines to meet."

I groaned, dropped my shoulders, and strode toward Mike, taking the package from his hands without making eye contact. I walked past Bryce with nothing more than a gust of air passing between us. "Come on."

Bryce stood still. "Don't we need gloves?"

"Come on," I repeated angrily.

We walked out through hangar doors then turned at the corner of the building. The exterior was smudged with mildew, and the once pristine brown brick had yellowed with age. The waning reflection of the moon provided small streaks of light behind the building. As we kept walking, dark-gray clouds loomed over the moon ominously, and the small tufts of ruined grass surrounding the back of the hanger were perished and brought to despair and darkness once again.

As we approached the wide-open space between the two hangars, Bryce followed the gravel path that led away from our hangar. I could hear the crunch of rock under his work boots.

"Owen, did you see this? This is a restricted area out here at the end of the airport."

In fact, I had seen the square, fenced area before. I never worried about it much.

Bryce charged ahead and squeezed through an opening in the rusted fence. He fiddled with a dilapidated iron latch.

"I wonder what's inside here. I can't believe UPS would put something like this here."

As I moved closer, I saw flecks of rust scattered on Bryce's fingertips. He rubbed them together, and they fell away.

He looked back at me, his eyes glistening. "The lock on the fence is rusted loose."

"Bryce, don't—"

"Shhh," Bryce insisted. "Listen."

I let a moment pass between us. "We need to get back inside."

Bryce brushed away my gesture, and then I heard it. A faint whisper that grew louder.

"Let me out. Let me out!"

Bryce looked back at me. "See. I told you I heard something!"

"Let me out." The voice sounded infantile at first but then became stronger and more resounding. "Please, let me out! Let me out. I've been in here for so long. Please, let me out."

Bryce reached forward and stuck his hand between the dark slat of space separating the door and the metal box.

"What are you doing?"

"Letting this person out, Owen. We can't just go back inside if someone has been locked in here. That's cruel."

I swallowed hard. "Bryce, don't—"

He slipped his hand inside and then yelped. "Something bit me." He jerked his hand back, and blood trickled between his fingers. Bryce shook his hand in a semi-circular motion and speckles of blood landed on my uniform.

The metal door swung back, and something bolted from the darkness and ran around the box. *"There I go. That way."*

Bryce stood up and dabbed his bleeding fingers on his pants. "What was that? Did you see it?"

I looked around. "No, just a dark flash, and then I heard the pattering of feet. It went around the back of the fence."

"We need to find out what it is," Bryce said. "I'll go around one side, and you go around the other."

I stepped back into the darkness. "No way. We need to get back inside and report this then get your hand bandaged."

"Not a chance," Bryce replied. "That person or thing attacked me, and I want to see it."

Bryce quietly slithered like a snake around the left side of the fence. I groaned and went to the right.

After a brief pause, the voice spoke again.

"It's going that way. That way."

As I ran back around the fence, I tripped over the leaking paint package and fell in front of Bryce.

"There I go. That way."

We scrambled to our feet. Suddenly, a motion light from the rear of the warehouse bathed our location in a soft hue of light.

Standing in front of us was a jackrabbit with antelope horns and a pheasant's tail. It reared back and sat on its haunches. Its thin lips quivered, and it spoke again.

"I'm going that way. Thanks for letting me out."

The rabbit leaped over Bryce and latched onto my shirt. The sharp horns burrowed through the fabric, tearing it while the tips of the horns jabbed into my flesh. Blood began oozing from the puncture wounds, and I screamed.

Instinctively, I grabbed the rabbit and flung him into the field beside the fence. I heard a thud then the rustling of feet again. The sound appeared to surround us.

"*There I go. That way.*"

Bryce stood motionless. "What do we do now?"

I heard nothing except silence and the occasional roar of planes taking off.

Something whisked by my ear and ricocheted against the fence. Before I had time to look, another small object hit the fence, then another. I smelled sulfur.

"What in the world was that?" Bryce stood up, and I shoved him down. Two more small objects missed us and hit the fence. Near Bryce's foot, I saw a shell casing.

"Come on, move!"

Bryce and I crawled around to the other side of the fence. For a moment, the shooting stopped. My heart banged against my chest wall, and my throat felt dry and hoarse. Bryce looked at me with clenched fists.

"*There I go. That way.*"

I stuck my head around the fence. The motion light had shut off, and the darkness was so thick the area behind the field merged with the sky. I couldn't see any protruding objects like a gun barrel in the darkness, so I crawled around to the left side of the fence, locking my fingers inside the metal holes to keep my balance.

I rose up for a moment, and another bullet zipped by me. A small wisp of smoke curled up from my shirt as I dropped to the ground again.

"*There I go. That way.*"

The pounding in my chest now resonated in my head. Behind me, Bryce slid to the opposite side of the restricted area, and I called out. "We are employees of UPS. Please, don't shoot."

"Shut up! You don't know who you are talking to."

Bryce looked sideways at the fence and then straight ahead. "I don't think the details are too important right now."

Ahead, I heard some movements. "Did you hear that?"

"No," he whispered.

I heard the muffled rustling again, and then another shot was fired. This time, the bullet clipped the top of the fence in front of Bryce. He collapsed flat on the ground and tucked his hands behind his head.

"Man, I'm getting scared now."

"Quiet."

The movement stopped. I held my breath, and Bryce remained motionless. The luminous moon glowed in the sky above. The rustling movements of what I presumed was the rabbit slowed down, and then they stopped.

"Bryce?"

"Yeah?"

"How fast can you run?"

I heard him swallow hard and cluck his tongue. "Pretty fast, I guess."

"Good. I have a plan. I am going to run in the direction of the shots and act as a diversion. I want you to run as fast as you can to the hangar and get help. Then come back. Got it?"

Bryce blinked at me twice, and he seemed to be grasping for the point of an anecdote that fluttered out of reach. "What if that horned rabbit attacks you again?"

Staring sternly into the pitch-black darkness, I found my eyes cautiously seeking out every detail in sight. "I'm not sure if it'll work, but I am out of ideas unless you have any."

"All right. One, two, *three*!"

I charged ahead into the darkness with my hands open, trying to feel anything in front of me. Something grabbed my wrists and pulled me further into what seemed like a dark abyss.

From behind, I heard a bump and a thud.

A pause ensued, followed by a shriek. I heard a grotesque squelching noise as Bryce screamed, "Get away from me!"

I pulled back at the large hands holding my wrists and shook one arm free. Before I could plant my feet, a punch hit my face, knocking me to the ground. From the corner of my eye, I saw the motion light on the rear of the building come back on, and another curdling scream echoed into the night.

The shadow standing over me was burly and slightly hunched. As it reached down to punch me again, I leaned up and rammed my head into it. The shadow stumbled backward, and I grabbed an arm and twisted it with all my strength. The cracking of bones punctured the air.

I scrambled to my feet as Bryce bounced toward me, gooey streams of blood running out of his nose.

He swiped the blood with the back of his wrist. "That rabbit tried to chew my nose."

"Are you going to be okay?" I asked him.

"Yeah." His eyes crinkled at the edges as he drew closer to me.

My skin felt hot, and I could feel pockets of flesh pulling together and protruding out from my face. "What the heck is that thing? That rabbit?"

A trim man with a mustache so neat it seemed penciled onto his face was lying on his back with one eye swollen shut and a large gash on his face. He wore camouflaged pants and an orange vest. We walked over to the man as he wallowed on the ground and moaned.

I grabbed him by the collar. His eyes flung open instantly, and his face gathered up in worry.

"Let me go, please." The man's voice was disarming.

I tugged more aggressively on the collar. "I don't think so. You tried to shoot my friend and me."

"I'm sorry," he said, the beginnings of tears shimmering in his eyes. "I was here hunting the jackalope."

I shot Bryce a disbelieving glance. "Jackalope? What are you talking about?"

He leveled a stare at me. "The jackalope—a rabbit with horns. The females produce milk that can cure all types of diseases. I heard rumors about one of them getting on one of these planes by mistake. I've been sitting out here at night for a few weeks. I think I've seen some of them darting back and forth toward that fence." He paused and nodded in the direction of the fence. "Recently, it sounded like one had been trapped inside that metal box inside that fence. I hope to kill it, milk it, stuff it, and then sell the milk for money."

I cut him off. "Do we look like rabbits to you? Why did you shoot at us?"

The man stammered, "I'm sorry. It was dark, and we couldn't see. The jackalope is fast, and if you don't take a shot when you think you have it, you'll never catch it."

I shivered with anger and adrenaline. "That...that jackalope attacked Bryce and me."

"They can be quite aggressive if they feel provoked or threatened," the man said.

"But we called out to you," Bryce interjected. "We told you we were UPS employees and what we were doing."

"Aw," the man replied in a fussy tone that reminded me of a child preparing to throw a tantrum. "With those planes taking off all the time, it's hard to hear sometimes."

The voice returned, silencing us. "*Thank you for letting me out. Now here we come.*"

"Stay still," the man commanded. "Let me get my flashlight." He turned into the darkness behind him and produced a flashlight and shined the light around us. Surrounding us were hundreds of jackalopes with their horns jutting from their skulls.

"*There we go. That way!*"

"Owen—" Bryce said, his voice trailing away.

I closed my eyes as the jackalopes leaped onto us and began stabbing and gnawing on our flesh.

As I struggled to dislodge them from my skin, pain surged through my body, and blood trickled from my arms. The blood began to pool on the ground in front of me. Then I heard a muffled scream as the swarm of jackalopes toppled Bryce to the ground.

"Help me!" Bryce bellowed.

The weight of the jackalopes began to drag me to the ground, and the pain of their teeth pulling at my skin was unbearable.

"*Here we come. There we go. We are going to put you in the box.*"

As I rolled over onto my side to reach out for Bryce, the jackalopes scurried ahead, carrying Bryce and the moaning man toward the box with their teeth.

"*There we go. There you go. Back in the box.*"

I began to lose consciousness as the screams of Bryce and the man echoed into the night.

Reckless

The inside of the truck smelled musty, a combination of mold and moist ragweed. Jonas stuck his head through the driver's side window, which he had rolled down at almost the exact second the evening highway patrol began. He took a deep breath, allowing the soft and hazy air to revive him. Then he retreated inside the truck and arched his back, temporarily forgetting about the decrepit truck. The late evening sunlight, rich and mellow, had brightened his mood for a moment.

Blinking against the glare, Jonas settled into the seat and tapped his fingers rhythmically against the steering wheel. After a few seconds, he stopped tapping and cut sharp looks to the left and right. Jonas flashed a sideways grin, loosened the seat belt, and leaned forward. Reaching an arm underneath the dashboard, he twisted and tugged at a small padlock with his thick fingers, then he heard the lock collapse onto the floor. Jonas pulled on a small latch where the lock had been, and the compartment sprang open. He removed a pewter flask from inside and gripped it tightly with his hand.

Jonas loved the flask and the feel of its polished finish and strong metal body. He held the flask in front of him, tilting it back and forth as the descending sunlight made the metal burst a gleam of silver across the stained, ruptured seat cushions. The swiveling movements of the flask revealed the engraved initials J.H. in Old English lettering. Nobody would mistake the flask as the property of someone else. This one belonged to Sheriff Jonas Holdren.

Jonas unscrewed the cap, clasped his lips around the opening, and tipped the flask back, greedily guzzling the vodka inside. The liquid wet his throat and made him shiver. Jonas laughed and tossed the flask onto the floor then wiped his shirt's sleeve across his chin, which was replete with some mildly roguish stubble.

Taking a quick check of the rearview mirror, Jonas resettled himself. He always enjoyed the fifth flask of vodka the most because it tasted the best. Jonas slung the seatbelt strap over his shoulder again, and the latch clicked inside the buckle. He reached for the portable radio lying on the seat next to him.

"Base, this is car one. Come in, base."

The whistling static pierced the silence inside the truck.

When several seconds passed with no response, Jonas sighed and pressed the talk button again. "Base, this is car one. Come—"

"I hear you, car one. You need to give a girl a minute to go to the bathroom."

Jonas stretched his legs, pressing the heels of his boots firmly into the floorboards of the truck. As he felt the front of the truck sag under the pressure, Jonas retracted his feet and groaned.

"Slow night, Dorothy?"

"No slower than usual," she replied sardonically. She burst into a coughing fit, and Jonas jerked the radio away from his ear almost as if to keep whatever microscopic germs may have traveled through the transmission from clinging to him.

"That's wonderful, darling."

"You just starting patrol?" Dorothy asked.

Jonas loved how her raspy voice hadn't changed over the years. She still sounded like she had smoked too many cigarettes, just had sex, or maybe just had her own shot of vodka.

"Nah, I've been at it for a few hours now. I'm sitting out here in a thicket of bushes on Highway 19 trying to catch speeders, but so far, all I've seen is a yellow Winnebago and Eric Flaherty's truck with a bunch of caged chickens."

"I hate chickens," Dorothy said placidly.

"But I like fried chicken," Jonas said, smacking his lips.

A moment of silence passed between them, only a faint rustling of static keeping the conversation alive.

As the vodka began to circulate throughout Jonas's body, he felt relaxed and slightly giddy at the same time.

He cleared his throat. "Where's Will?"

The static ended, and Jonas heard the faint ringing of a telephone in the background and Dorothy rolling her chair with its screeching wheels closer to the radio. Then there was an exhalation—the wheezing air making a sound like feedback across the channel.

"Will's in the back room processing speeding tickets."

"Tell him not to worry too much about them." Jonas released the talk button, but before Dorothy could reply, he pressed it again. "Oh, and tell Will to make one more pass through town before dark. It's Memorial Day weekend, and I don't want anyone from out of town getting any ideas."

"I'll relay the message."

Jonas flexed his shoulders and yawned. "All right, then. I'm going to make a couple of passes along the highway. I'll check in with you later."

Jonas went to toss the radio onto the seat, but Dorothy stopped him.

"Sheriff?"

"Yes." Jonas enunciated the word slowly.

"Congratulations on your retirement."

Jonas pumped the brake pedal with his foot and started the truck. "I'm not retired yet. I still have one more day of work left."

Dorothy snickered. "For goodness sake, you lazy SOB, you've been retired for a while now."

Jonas looked over his shoulder and down into the back seat. He squished the radio into his cheek and mashed his lips against the base as he strained to reach his wide-brimmed hat, which had fallen into the narrow space behind the passenger seat.

"You're on your way out, too, pretty soon." The words sounded mangled as he spoke.

Dorothy coughed. "Not for a while now. My daughter showed up at my doorstep two weeks ago with a baby and no place to go."

"Maggie?"

Another whistling of static came through the radio. "Yep. Maggie."

Jonas studied himself in the rearview mirror then nestled the hat onto his head, adjusting the brim so it rested just above both ears.

"Well, congrats, Dorothy," Jonas said, trying not to laugh at his own cleverness. He knew she'd mull over the statement, her emotions oscillating between pride and wondering whether he was messing with her.

The droning static stopped suddenly. "Base one, out."

Jonas shook his head and pulled the truck onto the highway. When he tapped the gas pedal, the truck cab shifted sideways, and the engine growled, its valves pinging rhythmically. The grinding and wheezing of the engine increased as Jonas applied more pressure on the pedal.

The alcohol gave him a resolved countenance. Jonas felt free, void of any need to maintain tact or adhere to established rules. He wanted to tell Dorothy that Maggie had been the town doorknob since she was sixteen and nearly every man had taken a turn. Maggie's sudden, unplanned pregnancy didn't surprise him, but he dismissed the thought, realizing the alcohol was thinking for him.

Jonas's heart beat harder, and small beads of sweat formed on his lips as the inside of the cab seemed to get warmer despite the crisp wind coming through the open window.

Jonas checked the mirrors then looked at the approaching horizon. The last bit of color was draining out of the sun as it crawled through a slightly cloudy sky, exploding in bursts of fiery orange and red before attempting to drop below the curvature of the earth.

He looked back to the highway and rubbed his eyes. He felt a bit woozy. The euphoric feeling created by the alcohol had begun to fade, so he reclined his seat, dropped his chin, and tipped his hat back with a finger. His eyelids became heavy, and two forceful head nods did nothing to shake the grogginess that overcame him.

As Jonas watched the odometer flicker, the truck hit a small divot in the pavement, causing the vehicle to rise up from the road. The jostling forced Jonas to grab the steering wheel tightly, but the truck began veering to the right. Jonas jerked the steering wheel to the left, and the truck steadied with the correction.

Jonas returned his seat to an upright position, and a gust of wind slapped a tangle of weeds onto the windshield. Jonas groaned and set the wiper blades in motion.

As the tattered and frayed blades pushed the weeds aside, Jonas caught the small, angular shadow of a person standing near the right edge of the road. Jonas screamed and slammed both feet against the brake pedal, sending the truck spiraling out of control.

He turned the wheel to the left then came back with a sweeping turn to the right, which lifted him off the seat and jammed his left side into the doorframe. The truck tilted onto two wheels and continued spinning. The acrid smell of burning rubber filled the cabin as Jonas tugged the wheel again and jammed the brake pedal to the floorboard with both feet, trying to slow down the swerving truck. Then Jonas heard a high-pitched squeal followed by the rear bumper slamming into something heavy.

The truck quit spinning and stopped.

Jonas shook his head and surveyed the scene around him. Everything inside the truck, including the papers and metal flask, were strewn throughout the cab. Thin streams of tire smoke curled inside and outside the truck. Jonas looked in the rearview mirror. A small cut had appeared under his right eye, but nothing in his body felt broken or torn as he eased forward.

Emerging from the truck, Jonas staggered back and forth, and frantic, haphazard thoughts darted through his mind as he struggled to find his balance. Jonas looked up and down the highway, and the road was silent except for a stiff wind that blew across the highway pavement.

Jonas walked around the truck, surveying the damage. The right bumper had a large indentation that had detached it from the frame and hooked it to the trunk lid instead. He ran a finger over the shards of metal, cutting a small hole in the tip of his finger. He pulled it back and sucked on it like a child nursing a bottle.

The wind increased, and Jonas squinted and turned away, trying to shield himself from being blinded by a collection of small rocks and highway dirt.

As he refocused, he saw what looked like a body resting on its side, facing away from the highway.

Jonas took a step closer then gasped at the tattered, light pink dress and beige shoes with ruffled, white socks. As he came closer to the young girl, he dropped to one knee and extended a trembling hand outward.

He slipped his fingers around her neck, checking for a pulse but found none.

"Jeez!" Jonas exclaimed as he stumbled backward, falling down on the asphalt.

He kicked himself away from the girl and spun around, trying to get up. He managed to rise to one knee, his head now spinning and throbbing. At that moment, all he wanted was another drink of vodka. He smacked his lips at the thought. He knew just one more little sip of vodka would calm him and help him make sense of the circumstances.

Jonas blinked hard, turned, and narrowed his gaze on the young girl. Sprawled on her side with her face turned skyward, she was tall and lean with straight brown hair, caramel skin, and an aquiline nose. The girl had small, beady eyes, now frozen and staring into the clouds as death seized her body.

Jonas looked around and saw no one. His head spun and his stomach churned quickly. Stumbling back to the truck, he flung himself into the seat and turned the key, unsure if it would start. When the engine hissed and finally turned over, Jonas exhaled a deep sigh of relief and spun the truck around.

He pressed the gas pedal to the floor once again, and the vehicle began speeding away. Reaching below the steering wheel, Jonas turned on the truck's emergency lights and sirens. He grimaced, looking back several times at the girl lying motionless in the road with small pockets of churned dust circling her body.

Jonas approached the end of Highway 19 even faster than he had anticipated. He looked at the impossibly twisted roads slicing through town and the intricately layered, candy-colored buildings that jutted outward and upward from the hills in town, and, for the first time, wondered if he'd be able to drive the whole way without hitting someone else.

But he made it.

The police station, with its sloped roof and small windows running the length of the building at the end of Central Avenue, had one light on, emitting a soft white glow through two of the windows. Jonas hoped it meant Dorothy or Will would be inside.

Jonas nearly fell out of the truck then flung open the station door, skipped up the three steps in the foyer, and raced down the hall.

The door of the office at the end of the hallway was slightly ajar.

Jonas stopped just before the entryway and bent down, resting his hands on his thighs. As Jonas wheezed and inhaled deep gulps of air, someone inside the office began to stir.

Jonas stood upright and entered.

Will Hudson, a big, handsome man wearing Levis and a gray blazer over a plaid shirt, blinked twice at Jonas. Will dropped his pencil and shuffled the property tax receipts together into a neat stack. "What's the problem, Sheriff?"

"We—we've got a situation on Highway 19." Jonas felt a lump form in his throat as he thought about the little girl. He covered his mouth with his sleeve and coughed. He wanted to puke. "Where's Dorothy?"

Will raised an eyebrow, and Jonas studied him for a moment. "She's on dinner break and will be back in about an hour."

Jonas moved uneasily side to side, shifting his weight from one foot to another.

"Is everything okay, Sheriff?"

"I'm not sure." Jonas reached behind his back, unhooked his gun holster, and shoved it into a space on the corner of his desk. "I was on patrol, and I—I found a little girl on the side of the road. I pulled over to investigate. She was dead." Jonas stopped speaking, trying to flush the terrible image from his mind.

Will leaned in, looking at Jonas through furrowed brows.

Jonas stared back. "Did you try to call it into Dorothy?" Will asked.

Jonas looked around the room. The craggy walls of the small office made Jonas even more uncomfortable.

"At first, I was stunned." Jonas tried grasping for the point of another anecdote that now fluttered just out of reach. "I wasn't sure if she was dead or not, so then I checked her pulse, but I found nothing. I—I tried calling Dorothy and got no answer."

Will raised his eyebrows. "That's funny. I've been here processing these tax receipts for the last two hours, and I didn't hear anyone trying to contact her on the radio recently."

Jonas rubbed the back of his neck. "Well, I know how hard you've got to concentrate on those receipts—which, by the way, are not due tomorrow."

A sly smile crossed Will's face. "I like to work ahead."

Jonas nodded.

Will said, "Do you want me to go and secure the scene? I can contact the county paramedics, as well."

Plagued by guilt and relief, Jonas agreed, "I want you to check it out, Will. I'll contact the ambulance. See if you can identify the girl, too."

Will pushed himself back away from the desk, collected the receipts, and placed them inside a desk drawer. He tipped his head at Jonas. "Congrats on your retirement, Sheriff."

Jonas shook his head. "I'm not retired yet."

"You soon will be."

Jonas poked a finger into the air in the direction of Will. "You've spent too much time talking to Dorothy."

Will stood up, his weighty frame and broad shoulders filling up the room. He patted the sheriff on the shoulder. "Be back in a few, Sheriff." He disappeared down the hallway.

Jonas looked around the office before staring up at the copper-colored circular rust stains dotting the ceiling. Then he removed his hat and plopped into the chair. The low-hanging ceiling light bathed the room in a soft yellow glow that made him sleepy.

Jonas jerked open some desk drawers looking for another portable radio. When he found one, it seemed lighter and blurrier than the one in the truck had been.

Jonas took out the radio, slammed the drawer shut, and settled back into the rickety wooden chair. Again, his eyelids felt heavy as the adrenaline pulsing through his body subsided, releasing its grip on his nerves.

The thought of the girl's twisted body lying alone made his head ache. How could he have rationalized the decision to drive away? But Will would secure the scene and take care of everything.

***

"Sheriff. Sheriff. Jonas, wake up!"

He felt someone jabbing his ribs with the rubber tip of a radio.

"Jonas, where's Will?"

The sleep-smeared images in the office came into focus as Jonas pried open his eyes. He looked sideways to find Dorothy's face resting inches from his.

"What? Will's not back yet?" Jonas replied, slowly drawing out the words.

"Back from where? Will was here working on receipts or something when I left, and then, when I come back, Will's gone, and you're asleep and snoring in his seat."

Jonas raised his head.

Dorothy leaned forward, her clenched fists resting on her hips. Her long, narrow face, beady brown eyes, and short nose made her appear rabbit-like.

Jonas sat up in the seat. Feeling something on his hand, he looked down to see small streams of spit had hardened on his skin. Jonas made a face.

"Yes, you drooled on yourself," Dorothy interjected.

Jonas scraped the hand on the edge of the desk while rubbing one eye with the other hand. "How long have I been asleep?"

Dorothy shrugged. "Beats me."

Jonas froze. "Where's Will?"

Dorothy shook her head. "We've discussed that."

"He should be back by now."

Jonas pushed the chair away from the desk and stood up, the muscles in his legs feeling weak and unsteady. He stretched, causing Dorothy to step back into the doorway where the milky-white light from the hallway divided her frame into uneven quadrants.

"Go back to the dispatch desk, and wait for me to call in. If you hear from Will, radio me and tell him to get back here." Jonas stopped in front of her as she blocked the doorway with both arms extended to both sides of the doorframe. Jonas dropped his jaw and glanced at Dorothy. "Dorothy, do it now."

She released one arm, and he slipped past her into the hallway.

He heard her mimic his words to herself as he came back into the room to retrieve his holster belt and adjust it around his hips. "And call the county paramedics, and tell them to meet me on Highway 19 near the fork in the road at Benders Creek."

***

Jonas drove through town, tapping the gas pedal on the truck frequently, and taking dangerous turns around cars parked throughout the tight, narrow downtown streets.

Highway 19 straightened into a flat, two-lane road. The steep hillsides, which were parched and dusty after the dry summer, sat back deep from the road. When Jonas maneuvered the truck close to the right shoulder, he could see jagged cracks shooting off into different directions as the earth split into fractious pieces like a jigsaw puzzle.

The truck engine roared loudly, and the cab rolled along with a slight hitch, one that Jonas attributed to the rear tires coming out of alignment during the accident. He reached under the seat in the truck and removed another small flask. Loosening the cap, he tilted the flask back and swallowed the warm vodka in one gulp. A small, errant droplet fell from his chin.

The accident. Jonas groaned to himself as he thought about that little girl. Hopefully, Will had secured the scene and was completing a report.

As Jonas passed Benders Creek, he saw the rear frame of Will's police cruiser on the side of the road, the lights still flashing. The rollers projected a hypnotic, sprightly pattern on the road, the only consistent illumination.

Jonas turned on his spotlights, pulled in behind the cruiser, and grabbed the radio, which had been catapulted to the passenger floorboard during the accident. "Base, this is car one. Come in, base."

Jonas pressed his lips tightly together after speaking, trying to cut any edginess or aggravation from his tone. "Car one, this is base. I'm here, Sheriff," Dorothy replied.

Jonas lowered his head, surveying the scene through the windshield of the truck. "Heard anything from Will?"

A brief burst of static came through the radio, followed by several long seconds of static. "No. Will hasn't radioed or come back."

Jonas gripped the radio so tightly in his hand he heard a knuckle crack. "Where are my paramedics?"

There was more static crackle before Dorothy answered, "They're on the way, Sheriff. ETA of ten minutes at the most."

"Thanks, base. Car one out."

Jonas opened the door and stepped out. The highway remained quiet as Jonas reached the periphery of the scene. The early evening sky, now well veiled in clouds, was occasionally darkened further by mist.

Jonas cupped his hands around his mouth. "Will. Will. It's Jonas. Where are you?"

He let the silence pool.

Jonas heard nothing.

He called Will's name again. "Will!"

Silence.

Jonas loosened a flashlight from his belt and shined it near the cruiser. Removing the revolver from its holster, Jonas cocked the trigger.

He slowly slid between the truck and the rear of the cruiser. A rustling noise came from in front of the car, and he stepped forward cautiously, turning the flashlight and pointing the gun toward the sound.

A raccoon reared back on its haunches and hissed at Jonas. The light and the presence of a human frightened the animal, and it scurried away. Jonas exhaled and began laughing stupidly at himself.

He turned around and sprayed the light around the road with long, sweeping strokes. Will was missing.

Then he saw the fingertips of a hand extending from near the left side of the car.

Jonas squinted.

He'd seen no sign of the girl yet. The fleshy fingertips had to be hers.

He walked around the front of the car slowly, still clutching the revolver in case of more wildlife.

Instead, Jonas saw Will's body, sprawled on his stomach, near the tire and nearly hidden under the police car.

"Oh, my gosh. Will!" Jonas jammed the gun back into the holster and set the flashlight down on the pavement, aimed toward Will.

The back of Will's skull had been smashed, leaving a deep divot above the base of his neck. The hair and skin were peeled away from the scalp, and blood oozed from the wound. Jonas waved away the flies that had begun circling the hole, only to find globs of pinkish-beige brain matter hanging through the open gap in the skull and slithering down the nape of his neck. The body smelled sweaty, a combination of salt and soured milk that Jonas felt sticking to his skin. Jonas reached for Will's neck to check for a pulse but found nothing.

Jonas secured the flashlight. Looking around, he saw two shell casings littered next to the body, which indicated Will had removed his gun and fired it. The sheriff reached for the gun and touched it, and then he pulled his hand back. The gun was still warm to the touch.

Something made an abrasive sound.

Jonas stood up and drew his gun, flashing his light quickly around him. A rush of adrenaline overwhelmed his body. If that raccoon had returned, Jonas would make sure it felt the wrath of everything that had happened that day.

The noise approached him.

Jonas turned slowly and moved around to the left side of the cruiser.

The little girl stood in front of him, horribly disfigured but very much alive.

Jonas screamed.

His legs trembled, and he held the gun tighter.

The girl stared at him blankly. Dark lines encased each eye up to her eyelashes, making the sockets seem bruised. In contrast, the sallowness of her skin created a sickly glow that hovered around her body, and she stood with her chest extended as if she were a puppet being manipulated by strings. In the light, her eyes glowed with a copper hue, and streams of fresh blood emerged from the corners of her mouth.

Jonas panted, struggling to get enough air into his lungs.

The girl took a step toward Jonas.

He directed the barrel of his revolver at her chest. "What did you do to my deputy?"

The girl cocked her head to the side and began twirling a loose strand of hair with her finger. "I'm so scared," she said in a high-pitched voice that was both soothing and disconcerting. "I want to go home. Can you take me home?"

Jonas steadied the revolver. "What happened to Will?"

"He was mean. He tried to hurt me. All I wanted was to go home, but he didn't want to take me. Will you take me?"

Jonas cut a sharp look at Will. The emergency sirens in the background were faint but coming closer.

"I need to help my friend." Jonas ran a rough tongue over his chapped lips. "He's badly hurt. As soon as I help him, then I will take you home, okay?"

The girl took another step closer. This time, her shoulders slumped, and she began trembling. "I want to go home now. Please, take me now."

"Listen, honey—"

"My name's not Honey. It's Miranda."

"Okay, Miranda. My friend is hurt and needs to go to the doctor. I need to help him."

Jonas paused. He traced the apparent glow surrounding the girl with his eyes, noticing it grew brighter with each passing moment.

"This is ridiculous. You're not even real. I hit you. I ran you over. You're supposed to be dead."

"I'm okay, Sheriff Holdren. Really, I am." She took two more steps toward Jonas.

His hands trembled more.

Miranda clenched her fists and lowered her gaze, her mouth fixed in an expression of moodiness.

Then Jonas saw a menacing look wash over her face. She opened her mouth, revealing jagged, lined teeth that resembled those of a shark. "Take me home!" she demanded, her voice now a loud, full-throated roar.

Jonas jumped back and fired the revolver.

A bullet missed her shoulder, and she flinched, grinned sadistically, and then kept coming at Jonas.

The sheriff sidestepped the police cruiser and leaped over the guardrail into the dusty fields near the highway. His left boot caught in a shallow hole in the shoulder pavement, and he stumbled and fell. Pushing himself up by the wrists, Jonas ran.

Puffs of dust rose around him, penetrating his nose and mouth. Jonas coughed, trying to clear his lungs while wiping his nose. After several minutes of running, a wide expanse of land lay in front of him. In the darkness, it became difficult for him to see how far he had run or where he was headed.

Jonas listened for sounds as he ran but heard nothing. He stopped.

Again, no sounds emerged from the darkness.

Finally, he turned around. Despite the skin crawling on the back of his neck, nobody was standing behind him.

Wiping the dust from his uniform, Jonas felt relief that he had outrun the little girl. "Pull yourself together, Jonas." The air had grown chilly, and the sheriff could see his breath as he spoke, "It's just stress—the stress of losing Will."

The words escaped into the darkness.

Jonas pulled out a handkerchief and wiped the sweat from his forehead.

A sudden impact knocked him to the ground, and Jonas felt the girl lock her fingers around his windpipe, squeezing hard.

"Take me home, Jonas. Take me home," she said in that demonic growl.

Jonas wheezed and gasped, trying to catch his breath as Miranda continued compressing his neck. Jonas gagged, nearly vomited, and then bit Miranda on the arm.

She let out a low howl and loosened her grip.

Jonas reached back, grabbed a tuft of her hair, and yanked it so hard she slid over his shoulder and landed on her back.

Jonas started to stand up to run back to the highway and his truck, but Miranda grabbed his leg and sank her teeth through his uniform into his calf.

Jonas wailed in agony, then kicked her away and tried to run, but he couldn't run with his injured leg. He couldn't even walk. All steadiness and power in his leg had disappeared, and large streams of blood ran from the wound.

Miranda leaped again, this time securing Jonas by the neck and twisted him to the ground.

Facing Miranda now, Jonas saw her eyes blaze a sharp gold color. "Reckless, Jonas. Reckless. Take me home."

She pinned his arms down to the ground, and he couldn't understand why she was so heavy. Jonas kicked and wiggled, and just as he began to slide away, Miranda bit Jonas on the neck.

He felt her sever the carotid artery, felt his life leaving him.

He tried to grab Miranda by the neck but found the strength in his arms had left. She tore into him, scratching large clumps of flesh, tissue, and muscles from his neck and throat. Then, suddenly, Miranda sprang up and ran into the darkness.

He'd thought he'd run a long way into the hills, but he was only a few feet away from the cruiser where he could see Will's hand under the car. He heard the screeching tires of the ambulance and doors slamming shut as the paramedics secured the scene.

When he heard the patter of footsteps approaching, he tried to speak, but no words came out.

A bright-eyed, baby-faced paramedic knelt over Jonas and pressed a white bandage onto his bleeding neck. "Sheriff, what happened to you?"

The blood in his throat rendered him unable to speak. He lifted a finger and waved it toward where Miranda had run. The young paramedic was becoming a hazy blur. *There. Look over there.*

"It's all right, Sheriff. There is nobody here. We heard a noise and looked around the field. The only people here are you and your deputy. That must have been some accident. It looks like you smashed his head right in when you hit him...when you lost control of the truck..."

Reflections

I closed my eyes and took a deep breath. The cemetery where most of my family members were buried, including my dad, lay before me. I missed my father, but I hated coming here to see him.

Standing in front of the cemetery gate, I looked to the east and watched the early morning sun fracture the hazy, humid August sky into a kaleidoscope of color with dark reds and fiery orange streaks of light and making a temporary imprint above the cemetery ridge.

I refocused on the cemetery gate in front of me. Stepping closer, I noticed the flecks of faded paint and rust dangling from the wrought-iron bars. Unlatching the gate, I stepped on the narrow, paved road and scanned the grounds. Seven erect tombs on the western side of the cemetery had inscriptions on the doors. I didn't know the people inside the tombs but imagined the lettering told their life stories. The tomb doors were opened, and debris rose up covering the entryway to most of them. The small, sloped cemetery had an aura of hallowed ground. I felt each grave held the life of someone important or someone who was special to someone else. I didn't feel this way until I stepped inside the gate and the entire cemetery was before me.

As I proceeded towards Dad's grave, the early morning humidity hung in the air like a thick wool blanket with its suffocating persistence and felt heavy in my lungs, forcing labored breathing. I looked around and observed other broken gravestones, some of them nearly one hundred years old. That side of the cemetery was the oldest section where many of the previous owners and caretakers of the cemetery of years past were buried. The graves were speckled with a granular substance, making them difficult to interpret or read.

The cemetery ground buckled slightly under my feet. I smelled nothing other than the thick, still, calm air. My steps grew slower and smaller as I approached the grave.

Finally, Dad's grave was visible. The flat, pewter headstone at the base of his grave was decorated with ornate marble lettering declaring this place to be his final resting place. The wispy grass under the headstone rose up in different directions. The nature and composition of the headstone gave the grave a regal appearance.

Sometimes, I felt guilty because Dad rested here alone. Mom was alone, too, resting comfortably in that nursing home under the attention of strange men and women who made sure she was okay. Dad would not want to be separated from her, and yet he was here without her, surrounded by the graves of other family members—some he knew well, some he never knew.

I dropped to my knees, and my hands trembled. My stomach soured. Sometimes, I needed medicine to calm my anxiety before coming to see him. Other times, I relied on alcohol to take away the sadness and other feelings I had, but neither seemed to make the trips to the cemetery easier for me.

Dad has been gone for five years, and I visit him at least once a month. I wondered if that was enough. How would Dad feel knowing I came to see him for just a little while one day out of the thirty or thirty-one days in each month? Then I thought about how often I saw Dad growing up. Maybe my guilt was displaced.

My dad was the only mortician in town, and he knew everyone. I could ask him anything about any family member in town, and he would tell me who their parents were, who they were married to, what they did as an occupation, and if their parents were still living. Dad put the community first, and they had loved him. Our home was filled at Christmas time with succulent, mouthwatering cakes, pies, and candies from many of the widowed women in town or the surviving children or grandchildren of the parents Dad helped bury over the years. They gushed about him to Mom and me, and we could never go anyplace without him running into someone we knew, not that we went out as a family very often.

Because of Dad's work, our house had a telephone in each room, including the bathroom. It would constantly ring, especially at night when a doctor, hospital, or family member placed the death call. Mom and I did a lot of activities together, just the two of us. Dad missed plenty of holiday dinners, Sunday church services, and many anniversaries because he was busy comforting grieving families. Sometimes, Mom and I would talk about Dad, and it was as if we were speaking about a mythical figure or someone from an urban legend. I never understood why Dad spent so much time away from Mom and me. He always said it mattered. When I needed Dad, he was at work. When Mom and I needed comfort, Dad was at work. When Mom had her stroke seven years ago, Mom was home alone when it happened because Dad was at the funeral home, comforting a sad mother who had just lost her son in a car accident.

I extended my hand and traced the letters of his name. My father loved cemeteries because of the serenity and respect they commanded. As a mortician, he brought so many families to these places. He often told me as a child not to be fearful of cemeteries for they kept our loved ones safe once they died. We came to this cemetery every year, sometimes twice each year, to lay flowers and wreaths at the graves of our family members. Dad would always trace their names with his fingers. He would wedge his plump index finger into the grooves of each engraved headstone and slowly slither his finger around every inch and turn of each letter. Dad always preferred prominent, emboldened lettering on headstones because he said it made them regal in appearance, compared to those with the routine carved letters, which he traced with the same care and attention. Dad always said tracing the letters would help you never forget their names and their importance in your life. Following that ritual, Dad would say a prayer, and then we would spend some 'silent time,' as he called it, remembering all the good memories of the deceased family. I'd knelt beside Dad, although I never could sit still because I wanted to look at the other graves and headstones.

I traced the letters on Dad's grave and completed the prayer and 'silent time' ritual just like he'd taught me. I normally saw other people doing something similar to my routine. As I began

The statement hung in the air for a moment. I couldn't speak. Instead, the smell of fresh dirt and lemons permeated my nostrils. I reached into my pocket, pulled out a handkerchief, and dabbed my runny nose.

"Um, can I help you with something?" I asked. I had not seen this caretaker before. A doughy-faced, stout younger man normally supervised the cemetery, but this caretaker seemed calm and confident, and he did not seem concerned about my presence or purpose for being here, which I found disrespectful.

He stopped moving again, then stepped back and turned on the balls of his feet. He faced me, and with narrowed eyes and thin lips pressed tightly together, he flared his nostrils in response. "I should ask you if I can help you with something."

I stepped back and furrowed my brow. I was in no mood for a game of verbal jousting.

"This is my father's grave," I replied confidently, assuming the man was in the wrong place.

"I know that, Mr. Bowen."

I blinked twice as he looked back at me.

His face softened, and as his eyes widened, I saw his steely blue pupils searching me, trying to ascertain my next move.

I cleared my throat. "How do you know my name?" I leaned in. "And who are you? I come here quite a bit, and I don't think I've seen you here at this cemetery before."

The man wore a faded, navy blue coat with both old and fresh dirt stains splattered across the surface and dark brown stains encircling the knees of his faded jeans. In his hand, he revealed a rag and a bottle, which he gripped tightly and kept by his side.

"I just came here to visit my dad," I said, sounding defensive.

The man nodded. The air had grown still again, and I thought I heard my words echo throughout the cemetery when I spoke.

The man slowly lifted his arms. I wondered what he might do next. Would he throw me out of the cemetery?

"My name is James, and I am the caretaker of the cemetery."

I felt a moment of calm overcome me while my cheeks burned with embarrassment.

"Each week, I come out and polish the tombstones. I start at the back and move my way to the front." He winked at me. "I start with your daddy's first."

"Why? There are so many headstones and graves in this cemetery, and some of them are in pretty bad shape. Why does my father get special treatment?"

"Because your daddy was a good man," he replied. "You might not know this, but a lot of the people buried here came here with your father." James scoured the cemetery and nodded in different directions. "The Madisons are buried over there, Henry and Mabel Hughart over there, the Millers just near the fence—"

"Wait," I interrupted. "I don't understand."

"Your daddy helped so many families say goodbye to their loved ones," James said, pressing his lips together. "He was especially kind and helped comfort so many people. Also, those people I mentioned, your daddy was here when we buried them. He was here with their families to comfort them." James stood back and looked me up and down. "Yep, you were too young to remember a lot of it."

I froze under James's comments. Dad was familiar with this cemetery, and that was why he didn't feel totally uncomfortable bringing me here. Our biological family members were buried here, but so were the extended family members of people Dad helped through the funeral process for so many years.

James watched me closely as these thoughts raced through my mind. "I still don't understand, though, why you choose his headstone first?"

"He's worth it."

For the first time since we talked, James stepped aside, and I looked at the tombstone. The granite headstone glinted with a rich black hue in the sunlight. The block letters with my dad's name sprawling across the headstone appear polished, and their new look gave them a feeling of royalty as if a king resided here.

My mouth agape, I didn't know what to say. Transfixed on the clean, shiny headstone, I forgot James was still beside me.

I looked back at him, ready to thank him for his kindness. Instead, he just nodded and flashed an impish smile.

"Come with me."

James walked away from me and headed to the middle of the cemetery, a mere thirty yards from Dad's grave. He dropped to his knees and began the same rhythmic swivel motion I'd witnessed earlier.

We came upon two shallow graves with two flat, rectangular headstones. The metal was chipped, and the lettering identifying each plot had faded some. A small bug crawled over the chipped edge of the tombstone. The insect minded its own business, but its presence apparently bothered James because he flicked it away. From behind, the sunlight encased James in malevolent strands of golden light.

James pointed down at the graves. "My mommy and daddy are buried here," he said, his voice sounding knotted. "I lost them both at one time in a car accident. I thought I wouldn't make it through the funeral. When they put their caskets into the ground, I fell down and cried for hours. Your daddy stayed with me until I was ready to leave. I reckon we were here for about five hours or so after the funeral."

He looked back at my dad's grave.

"Your daddy didn't say much to me, but as an only child who had lost my parents, I knew I wasn't alone and that someone wasn't going to leave me alone. He took care of me, and I will always make sure, as long as I'm responsible for these grounds, to take care of him."

At that moment, I realized my father would never be alone in this place. James would not allow it.

Snapshots

A noise came from the living room—a vibration and a disconcerting rattling like a wounded animal trying to escape.

Grimacing, Blake lay in bed, arms and legs extended outward from his body like a starfish. Beside him, the flat, dull hum of the computer fractured the otherwise still silence of the bedroom.

Blake pulled himself up, groaning as muscles in his back tightened. He rubbed his swollen eyes with the knuckles of both hands. Sleep-smeared, he blinked hard—twice. The ornate clock mounted on the wall read 4:18 a.m. He took a long look at the wad of cash, coiled around a stack of folded and torn envelopes with bills jutting outward from the tattered edges, sitting on the nightstand. Blake stroked the money like it was a family pet.

Ava should be with me, he noted. Blake missed her pint-sized curves and those serious, green eyes. Only she could soothe this insomnia.

Stumbling through the cluttered bedroom, littered with piles of clothes, towels, and empty beer cans, Blake reached into the closet. Pushing aside some scattered clothes, he snatched a small, locked metal box and frantically twisted the numerated dial, struggling to remember the combination. The noise grew louder. Blake went back to the nightstand, grabbed the cash, and stuffed it into the box before locking it again, then he put it back on the closet floor and covered it with some discarded shirts. Blake grabbed a baseball cap and worked a sweatshirt and low-slung jeans over his naked body. He moved with languorous authority into the living room, which mirrored the conditions of the bedroom.

The rattling in the living room accelerated into a frantic vibration. Blake walked across the room then paused and watched intently as the front door wiggled and wove slightly inside the frame as the rattling intensified. Clenching and releasing both fists, Blake reached for the knob and pulled the door open.

Ava stumbled and steadied herself with one hand inside the entryway while gripping a small silver key. "Dang it, Blake, I'm so sick of always having to spend ten minutes trying to unlock this decrepit door!" Ava's milky skin illuminated the dark room. Her eyes flickered wickedly.

A strangled smile etched Blake's face. "If anyone would know how to do it right, it would be you." Blake yawned. "What are you doing here anyway? I thought your shift lasted until six?"

"It's been slow tonight, so the captain let me go." Ava marched past Blake, and a sample of the September weather, heavy and close, seeped into the room behind her.

Ava shoved piles of old newspapers away and collapsed onto a faded brown couch underneath a sloped window.

Blake offered coffee, which Ava refused.

"I have some of the information you requested." Ava stood and glared out the window onto the city skyline.

As Blake turned on an overhead light in the kitchen, Ava watched his movements closely. Then Blake moved closer.

Something in her jaw tightened as she removed a small notepad from her pocket.

"Before we talk, Ava, and since I'm up, why don't we do this over some breakfast and coffee at Smiley's?"

Ava set her jaw. "Fine, but we need to be careful."

Blake nodded. "I agree, but I don't think the people we're worried about seeing us will be hanging out at Smiley's Diner in the middle of the night."

Blake moved closer to Ava, wanting to embrace her and feel her body pressed against his own, but when Blake reached out an arm to ensnare Ava, she moved to the door.

"Let's go," she commanded, her voice firm but stoic.

They agreed to walk on opposite sides of the street to Smiley's Diner to ward off suspicion from anyone who might be watching. Even though Blake lived in the Flats just outside downtown Cleveland, he knew cops and, potentially, friends of Ava would still patrol these areas late at night. The low-lying topography of the Flats rested tightly against the banks of the Cuyahoga River. Smiley's Diner was located in Irishtown Bend, which extended from West 25th Street east to the river north of Detroit Road. The late-night fog was thick, so the tops of the warehouses and buildings in the Flats merged with the dark sky overhead.

Ava's figure faded into the fog for a moment but reemerged as Blake crossed a deserted West 25th Street and closed in on her and the diner.

Smiley's Diner was a flat, elongated, and faded white building with a sloped awning and two large glass windows, which allowed customers to look toward downtown Cleveland. The diner had been a machine repair shop for the cargo ships that roared up and down the Cuyahoga River collecting steel from the mills during the 1930s and 1940s. Now, Smiley's served as the only twenty-four-hour restaurant option for the tenants that occupied the newly constructed warehouse apartments that now occupied the abandoned industrial buildings.

Inside, Ava sat at a small booth near the back of the diner. When Blake walked in, he noticed that Smiley's was basically empty. Ava waved at Blake, signaling him to come and sit down. He passed a table messy with the remains of dinner, a pair of flies making disorganized swoops and arcs over the plates. The faded wooden tables and chairs were spaced evenly throughout the room, sometimes resting awkwardly against the chipped, white and black tiled floor. The worn booth benches and tables were set tightly against the windows running the length of the left wall.

Blake sat down hard onto one of the booth benches.

Ava dug through her jacket pocket while Blake studied her. Ava's lithe frame and small brown eyes seemed to envelop the entire booth. He watched the tiny pockmark on her forehead crinkle as she searched for her notes.

"Okay," Ava said, sucking in a breath. "From what I read in the detective's notes, your brother Lance has been missing since last Tuesday. We searched the apartment, which was ransacked when we got there." She paused, brow furrowed. "No traces of fingerprints or hair, but they did find an unused needle and syringe in the bathroom that will be tested."

Ava closed the notepad and tossed it on the table. "I'm not the lead detective on this case. Mike Roth is handling the investigation, and if he knew I was sharing information with you about it—"

Blake knew what Ava was doing for him put her in a bad position. He remembered the first time he crossed paths with her at the police station. He had been searching through the arrest reports, looking for information to include in the police blotter section for the paper the next day. She charged confidently into the records room, and her beauty and intelligence—and the fact that she had a calm reticence, which still impressed him—had immediately intrigued Blake.

Blake nodded. "I know the risks you're taking by doing this for me. I really had nowhere else to turn." He wondered if her concern also stemmed from their secretive romantic relationship, but Ava looked away for a moment.

Ava, her posture tense as if she were perched on the edge of a doctor's table awaiting a physical examination, crossed both arms. "The fact that he is on the run from us now makes four brushes with the police in two years. That is not good news for your brother."

The conversation was interrupted by the appearance of a pert and trim waitress who dipped a dishrag into a pan of soapy water and proceeded to wipe the table, causing Ava to grimace as flecks of water moistened the end pages of her notebook. The waitress then dumped the rag back into the pan and set it on a wooden chair behind her. She pushed back the brown hair overhanging her brow. The powder-blue polo shirt and white skirt she wore were splotched with grease and sauce stains.

"What can I get you to eat or drink?"

"I'll have coffee, black. No cream or sugar," Ava said. Despite being a cop who had to take command of situations, Ava had a beautiful voice, precise and smooth.

Blake felt his stomach lilt and growl. He thought for a moment and then met the gaze of the waitress. She stared back at Blake with a sour expression softened by experience.

"I'll have the pancakes with two eggs—scrambled—and two sausage patties, and I would like my coffee the same as hers."

The waitress nodded and disappeared.

Blake refocused his attention on the conversation. "I'm not even sure Lance will care," Blake said. "The smack is what matters to him. The risks and problems that come with it, he never considers important."

Ava stiffened. "You never mentioned Lance or his problems before last week. Why?"

Blake leaned back into the seat, swallowing hard. "Lance is not exactly the first or best topic of conversation when you first see someone you care about. I don't want you to always associate me as coming from a family of felons. The relationship that I've had with my brother was not always tenuous."

The waitress returned and set the cups of coffee in front of them. Before she could speak, Blake snatched the cup and tossed it back. The coffee, smooth and warm, did not relinquish the cold chills running through him. Talking about Lance worked under Blake's skin like a tattoo needle—the impression always indelible.

"Be back in a bit," the waitress said.

Blake leveled a look at Ava as she grabbed the notepad and stuffed it into her jacket pocket.

Blake thought about Lance. As the younger brother, Lance was always impatient and volatile. Blake tried to instill in Lance the importance of responsibility and self-respect. Instead, Lance always found that having a "good time," which included taking and dealing drugs, was more important, no matter what the cost or who was hurt in the process. For most of Lance's adult life, Blake felt contempt for him. The fact that Lance stayed in trouble and disrespected authority entirely while others made excuses for his behavior roiled Blake.

"He's screwed up so many second chances," Blake said.

Ava pursed her lips and leaned forward slightly.

"Lance got involved with some bad people, and I knew they had a lot of influence. He would call me and tell me that he was in trouble—" Blake felt his lips tremble as his voice trailed off. "This last group he was hanging with… some of them had been arrested and some killed in shootouts with the police. I wonder if he's found a new group."

Gathering himself, Blake peered at Ava and found her arms now uncrossed while leaning closer to him with an expression both wary and challenging.

"What will happen to him this time?" Blake asked.

"He's been developing a pretty sophisticated drug ring. We've caught some of the low and mid-level guys in his operation, but we want the big fish, and this time, we're going to get him! *When* we catch him, he will be held until arraignment." Ava let the words settle for a moment. "Aren't you familiar with how it works? He's been booked before."

Blake lifted the coffee cup to his lips again. He didn't look at her as he thought about all of the previous arrests. Blake shivered. The memory of the inside of courtrooms and watching his brother dragged in with chains and shackles around his wrists and ankles made Blake cringe. He had written statements to the judges and pleaded for leniency for Lance with several different prosecutors, but those instances were minor drug offenses, and the judges felt Lance could be redeemed and become "a productive member of society." Now, with the more serious pending charges, Blake wanted to stay away.

"Maybe this arrest will be the last."

Blake looked around the empty diner. The crescent-shaped counter was nestled against the kitchen wall where meals were prepared and slid through a metal port in the wall. Blake watched as a plate of food was pushed through the slit.

Ava placed a closed hand in the middle of the table. "You can't go back and undo what has already been done. Your brother is an adult, and he's responsible for his own choices. But you need to understand that he has a devastating addiction to drugs and money, which drives every action, thought, and motivation. I've worked enough of these cases to see the patterns in the behaviors of users *and* dealers. The links between drugs and crime are real. If you were so concerned about him, you should've got him some help a long time ago. There are plenty of good public and private rehab services that might've helped."

Ava paused. "Now it doesn't really matter. Lance will most likely go to prison because of the decisions he's made. You need to be prepared for that."

Blake looked sideways. "I don't know if I can help him, especially if he's sent to prison first."

Ava unclenched her fist and splayed her long, thin fingers across the table.

Blake quickly looked around the diner. Seeing nobody, he reached out, grabbed her hand, and pulled it to his cheek.

It smelled fresh and earthy like early morning summer dew. Blake nestled his cheek into her hand. Her skin, smooth and creamy, felt cool and familiar against his face. "I've missed you," he whispered.

Blake crossed an ethical line when he pursued a romantic relationship with Ava. Their meeting inside the police station unearthed an idea that could solve two purposes—he could be intimate with her, and she could help his family—so Blake made sure that he courted Ava privately, away from the police station and the newsroom. The newspaper had strict rules about reporters becoming romantically intertwined with their beat sources. Blake knew to be careful, and he had been, but the punishments could be severe—Blake could lose his position as a senior reporter at *The Plain Dealer* and be relegated to writing soft feature stories about church luncheons and family reunions in the community—but so far, everything was working.

As Blake closed his eyes for a moment, the waitress cleared her throat before setting a plate of eggs and sausage in front of him. "Are you ready to eat, or should I give you a moment?" The tone in her voice was hard and edgy.

Blake released the grip. "No, no. I'm fine. Thanks!"

The waitress rolled her eyes as she left again.

Ava ran her hands through her hair. "I need to know—when did you last see Lance? I know he's wanted to meet up with you several times before, and you've refused."

Blake, momentarily stunned at the change of circumstance and tone, stumbled in collecting his thoughts. "I told you—last Tuesday. He wanted to meet at the Tower City Mall, and I agreed. That's when I called you. I was late filing a story, and by the time I got to the mall, your cops had set up a perimeter, and Lance was gone. He must have sensed something was up and that the police were there."

Ava stared at the soft slatted moonlight streaming into the diner through the fog. The light, slowly fading, made the room a bit darker as dawn approached.

She turned back to Blake and cocked her head. "So you haven't met him, and now he's gone missing? Any idea where he might or could go?"

Blake arched an eyebrow. "Why do I suddenly feel like I'm being interrogated here?"

A cell phone rang. Blake had totally forgotten about it. The phone rang again, and Ava cast a long look at Blake as he lifted the handset to his ear.

"Hello," Blake said, dropping his voice and faking sleepiness.

"Are you asleep?"

Blake guffawed. "I'm not anymore, Mother." Blake glanced at the stack of pancakes with slathered butter running down the edges. "Mother, why are you calling me so late?"

A pause. "It's only past one a.m. here in Sacramento. Besides, I couldn't sleep. Have you heard from Lance?"

"Not since last week, Mother."

Then silence. Blake could practically hear his mother's thoughts racing across her mind.

She cleared her throat, raspy and deepened now from years of smoking. "I know your brother has done this before, Blake, but he's never just disappeared like this. I thought by now, he would have contacted one of us."

Blake held the phone receiver against his neck and settled in for what could be a long conversation. He watched as Ava stabbed a sausage link with a fork and stuffed it into her mouth. She glanced again at Blake with a studied reticence that Blake interpreted as a pitying stare.

Blake made a face and turned away from Ava, focusing again on the phone.

"Lance would contact you before he would contact me," Blake remarked.

Blake's mother dismissed the comment. "I got a letter yesterday from Nashville. I thought maybe it was from your brother. The letter was nothing more than a thank-you card from my neighbor for watering her plants. She's visiting family there."

Blake dropped his head. His mother had always been the one in the family who looked away from Lance with regards to his problems and his arrests. She would pretend they didn't exist. Lance sought their mother because he realized she had a fondness for him that would allow her to forgive and forget while enabling him to continue his reckless behavior. The thought still filled Blake with a quiet fury.

Blake heard his mother shift the telephone from one hand to the other, carefully mulling over a response.

Blake gleaned the disappointment in his mother's voice. "Lance will contact you when he needs money. He always does."

"Blake, you hurt my feelings when you state those lies."

Rage swelled up inside him. "Lies? Really, Mother? Then explain to me why every time the three of us were together during holidays, birthdays, heck, even when we were growing up in the same house, Lance always asked you for money, and you gave it to him again and again. Did you ever ask him why he needed that much money?"

"Lance wouldn't have asked me for it if he didn't need it."

"Good grief, Mother. I pointed out the marks on his arms. You remember what you said to me?"

Silence.

"Let me fill in the blank for you. Zits. You said Lance had a bad case of zits. Lance is an addict, Mother—an addict! You always expected me to set an example for him, and I have tried my whole life. I have tried to be the real man in this family. A son to you, and a brother to Lance. Then the one time I step up and try to have a real conversation with you about his drug use, you don't want to talk about it. It's been that way forever. No matter what, Lance gets an excuse for everything he does. This time, he has run out of excuses and run out of people who believe the excuses!"

Blake heard the voice of his mother shrivel a bit. "You and your brother always had oily skin growing up."

Blake took a deep breath, ready to respond, but his mother cut him off.

"His absence, what it's doing to me—"

Blake felt a pang of nausea settle in the pit of his stomach. He wanted to seize his mother—a chubby biddy with a waxen complexion—by the throat.

"Lance's absence? What it's doing to you? Have you considered what this is doing to me, Mother? You are on the other side of the country. I'm the one who is here and the one who has to answer all the questions and clean up all the mistakes while you get to be the casual observer, watching all of this from afar like it's a home movie."

The waitress weaved her way across the diner again and stopped at the table. Thrusting both hands on her hips, she arched an eyebrow at Ava before giving a disapproving glance at Blake. Ava bent forward and furrowed her brow. Blake hadn't realized his voice had reached a loud octave, but he knew she was listening carefully and gauging his reaction. The waitress took Ava's empty coffee cup away.

"Is she there?"

"Who, Mother?"

"Your detective friend."

"It's none of your business."

"She is there," his mother said confidently. "You always get so defensive when I ask about her. Can your friend help us find Lance?"

Blake exhaled a deep breath.

Ava looked down, fumbling with her holster belt, and said, "I'm going to the bathroom. Be right back. Looks like you need a minute."

Blake waited until Ava was across the diner before speaking again. He dropped his voice to a whisper. "I think so, Mother. But I am interested in more than her occupation."

"Be upfront and honest with her, Blake," she reminded him.

Blake had never been honest with women, mostly because he lacked the self-confidence to trust others. His job as a police and courts reporter for the newspaper forced him to trust other people as sources for story information and quotes, yet he never could trust people outside of work. Part of that was Lance's fault, and the other reason was too many failed relationships with women. Ava was different—at least, he hoped she was different.

Blake heard the metallic click of a cigarette lighter in the background, then his mother inhaled and exhaled deeply, sending static through the phone line. "She'll find Lance."

"If there is one thing this family has a problem with, Mother, it's honesty and reality. Good night."

Blake withdrew the phone from his ear just as his mother started to say something else. As Blake disconnected the call, Ava returned and stood in front of him, withdrawing a small, black radio from against her ear.

"I just heard some chatter on the radio. A patrol car found a car abandoned near a rest stop on I-70. They ran the plates, and it's Lance's car. A forensic team is on the way. I probably should go. Mike will want me there."

Blake stood up and slid his arms over her slender shoulders. "When can I see you again?"

Ava cut a sharp glance around the diner and flashed a pained expression. "I don't know, Blake. We've got to be so careful."

Blake nodded. "I know. You're right. I just want this whole thing to be over. Soon."

As Ava slipped away and walked out the door, Blake sat down again.

The waitress came back to the table and set the bill down on the edge. "Date night over so soon, eh?"

Blake groaned. "Yeah, something like that." He pulled out a twenty-dollar bill and placed it on top of the ticket. "Keep the change."

Blake watched the waitress scoop up the money and skip across the diner, disappearing behind the counter and nearly squealing with excitement. As Blake slid across the seat, digging through his pockets for the apartment keys, he rested a hand against the glass. In the background, he heard a train clacking down the tracks, creating enough vibrations that the walls in the diner shook slightly and his hand quivered against the pane.

Blake found the keys, and as he picked up the cell phone, he noticed the email icon on the screen flashing, indicating a new email had arrived. Blake looked at the clock on the phone. It read 7:31 a.m. Blake slid away from the window and swallowed hard.

When Blake moved a thumb over the blinking icon and opened the email, several photos of Ava and him appeared, all taken from a distance. The most recent pictures showed them entering the diner earlier and then talking to one another in the booth by the window. The biggest and best photo, an elevated snapshot, showed them standing next to the table at Smiley's before Ava left to find Lance's car.

Blake felt a trickle of sweat bead on his forehead and sighed. *Ava can't see these pictures.* Blake deleted the email.

Feeling the muscles in his face tighten, Blake covered his mouth with his fingers and groaned softly, then bolting up from the booth seat, Blake rushed to the front door of the diner.

"Is everything all right, sir?" the waitress asked from across the diner.

Blake ignored her and left the diner but stopped outside the front door. His hands trembled as he secured the phone, but Blake pushed the numbers and tightened the grip around the phone.

A taut voice answered on the first ring. "Yeah."

"Lance," Blake said. "It's me. I just talked to Ava, but apparently, you already know that based on the email I just received."

Lance let out a full-throated, heavy laugh. "It's called leverage. It keeps everything moving forward. I just wanted you to know that I'm around. Abandoning my car at the rest stop will eventually let the cops know I'm still around, too."

Blake pressed his lips tightly together. "Listen, the police... they've found your car. They're on the way to get it. I'm afraid she is going to find out what's going on."

Blake let the words resonate for a moment and thought about the money. Ava's concern over their relationship washed over him as beads of sweat dappled his forehead.

"Consider that wad of cash in your apartment as some snack money to tide you over for your time and… *expertise*. Now I have some questions for you about dear ol' Ava and how close to finding me the Cleveland PD is. It's tough being a sophisticated and profitable drug peddler when the police are always after you."

The fact that Lance was in control made Blake shiver in anger, but Blake gathered his composure. "All right, Lance, what do you want to know?"

Special Needs

Rhonda Pendleton closed her eyes as she remembered the day the state of West Virginia decided to lock her up in solitary confinement for two years because she had a rash.

Rhonda wasn't violent, and she hadn't threatened anyone. She was free on bond when she walked into a courtroom in Kanawha County in September to answer charges of selling prescription painkillers, which was a violation of her probation on a similar charge.

During the hearing on that bright, crisp Friday afternoon, when it looked like she was headed to jail, her lawyer revealed a secret to the judge.

"Your Honor, my client is sick," Ken Fillmore stated matter-of-factly before the court.

The judge leaned over the laptop computer adorning his desk and narrowed his eyes into slits. "With what, Mr. Fillmore?"

Ken stood up straight and cleared his throat. "With Hepatitis C, Judge. It's an antibiotic-resistant staph infection—"

The judge waved a dismissive hand. "I know what Hepatitis C is, Mr. Fillmore. Don't humor me."

The judge leaned back in his seat, the dark robe billowing away from his portly gut, and glared at Rhonda before settling a hard look back on Ken.

"Given this new information, I will be sending Ms. Pendleton to a *special needs* facility that can handle her situation."

Rhonda gasped, drawing another glare from the judge.

Ken looked down at his client, hunched over the table with her hands folded. The thumbs of her fingers weaved and slapped against each other in some nonsensical rhythm. Ken saw the beads of sweat collecting on her brow.

Ken cupped a hand on her shoulder, trying to relax his client. "Will Ms. Pendleton be able to receive treatment for her condition at this facility?"

The bench shielded the judge's less flattering proportions as he squared his broad shoulders and flashed an icy blue gaze on the room.

"I am going to send Ms. Pendleton to a facility that can handle her situation."

Ken clucked his tongue. "And this facility, Judge, it will be a place where my client can receive treatment?"

The judge took in a slow breath. "Yes. She is going to get treatment."

"Judge, my client—"

"Be quiet, Mr. Fillmore. I'm not through."

Rhonda felt pools of sweat permeating under her clothing in every conceivable crevice. She tossed her gaze between the judge on the bench and the attorney standing beside her. It felt like both men were volleying a tennis ball back and forth waiting for the other to make the final heavy stroke with the racket.

The judge ran a hand through his wiry, gray hair. "Would the defendant please rise."

Rhonda nodded.

Lisa shook her head and spoke to her notes. "First, the hearing in front of Judge Duncan lasted literally two minutes. Then they send you here, lock you down for twenty-three hours a day, allow you three showers a week, and feed you through a slot in the cell door. Ridiculous."

Lisa sat up straight, pushed the notepad away from her, and folded her hands, resting her wrists on the notepad.

"Rhonda, this is a relatively new law that we are dealing with here, and it's taking all of us some time to get used to it. Placing you, and others like you, in places like this helps alleviate a financial burden for the counties in the state that pay regional jail bills. The problem is the state did not define a formal review process for when inmates like you can be returned to the appropriate regional jail close to the county in which they live."

Rhonda grew impatient. "So when do I get out?"

"It's not that simple," Lisa said, biting off her words before going further. She pressed her lips into a thin line. "Rhonda, I understand from the warden that you attacked a guard who was removing you from your cell. Why?"

Rhonda sat up straight. Her gaze crossed Lisa's face before the features of her attorney hardened.

"That guard was going to take me outside into the prison yard." Rhonda looked down at her hands, feeling a pang of earnestness wash over her. "I was so scared. I didn't want to go outside into the yard. I had no idea what was going on, who was out there, or what they wanted me to do. I refused to go, but that guard, the witch!" Rhonda saw Lisa flinch at the comment, and she decided to collect herself. "That guard. She pulled me. Pushed me. Got some other guard to drag me out there. I felt like a bag of trash. Not like a person at all."

Lisa remained stoic and composed. "Is that the truth?"

Rhonda huffed and flopped back against the seat. "Of course, it is."

"Rhonda, if you lie to me, I can't help you."

Rhonda felt her stomach seize with anger, and the muscles in her neck tighten. "I am telling...*the*...*truth*!"

Lisa nodded. "Right."

A moment of silence fell between them. Lisa turned around and motioned to one of the guards. Lisa cleared her throat and closed the notepad. Then she clicked the top end of her pen on the table, the pointed end retreating inside the plastic tube. As the guard approached, Lisa's eyes met Rhonda's confused face.

"I'll be in touch."

Rhonda bolted up from her seat, causing the guard to take an aggressive stance. His hand grazed the baton case on his utility belt.

Lisa looked back casually at Rhonda. "Relax, Rhonda."

"Screw that. You just got here! We ain't talked but for a few minutes." The pitch in her voice was high and nervous.

With a finger, the guard motioned for Rhonda to sit down, and she did, refusing to take her eyes off Lisa. Once the guard stepped back, Lisa spun around on a heel.

"I know that, but I have other clients." She paused and stepped closer to the table. "As a public defender, you are just one of the dozens of cases I am responsible for. I mentioned that to you several times when the court appointed me as your attorney."

"I know what you said." Rhonda huffed, folding her arms in pouting defiance. She pursed her lips, and Lisa leaned over the table.

"I promise we'll talk again soon. In the meantime, no more fights with guards, inmates, or anyone else. Understood?"

Rhonda looked away.

Lisa arched an eyebrow as the guard placed a hand around her elbow. "I mean it, Rhonda. Tell me you heard me?"

Rhonda slammed her hand against the table. The thwack of skin against the surface made a loud sound that hushed the thrum of conversations in the room for a moment.

"Yeah, I heard ya."

Satisfied, Lisa looked at the guard and chinned her head to the door. In a few steps, Lisa Escue disappeared into the shadows.

Rhonda shook as the heavy steel door slammed shut behind them.

She recalled everything Lisa had told her during a previous meeting about her situation. To get Rhonda released, Lisa would petition the Lakin jail administrator to send a petition to the Kanawha County prosecutor in Charleston, saying that she had unmanageable issues or "special needs"—Rhonda hated that term. Then the prosecutor would apply for a court order to transfer Rhonda, and a judge would have to approve the request. Most likely, it would be Judge Duncan.

Thinking about his name made the bile rise in her throat. She hated him and Ken Fillmore for putting her here and leaving her without *due process*. At least, that was the term Rhonda remembered hearing Ken and Lisa utter several times.

As she was led from the visitor's area back to the cellblocks, Rhonda swayed back then to the side, then back and forth, balanced by the firm latex-gloved grip of a female guard grabbing the bend in her arm. Rhonda looked up and saw they had passed the entrance to Unit 3, her usual cellblock unit. Rhonda stopped moving, forcing the female guard, a squat and narrow-shouldered butch of a woman, to almost fall as the chain connecting the wrist shackles to the leg shackles got tangled in her boots.

When the guard spun around and aggressively charged Rhonda, she called out. "Where are we going? This ain't my cellblock."

The guard's face twisted into an ugly smirk. "Let's go."

"No. Not till I'm told where we are going."

The guard sneered an inaudible groan and reached for the baton on her belt. Rhonda's eyes followed her hand, and her instincts and a pulse of fear stumbled her forward. The guard removed the baton and placed her hand back in its previous location, the grip harder and firmer than before.

Rhonda stumbled forward as the guard made a grand gesture with her arm. At the end of the corridor, a guard hidden behind a concrete wall encased with a Plexiglas window nodded and pulled a lever. The steel door groaned and whined as it slid back on its hinges. The guard removed the shackles from her wrists and legs, and before Rhonda could say or do anything else, the guard shoved her inside. The gate made its slow trek back to the left, clicking shut with a loud thud, a sound that reverberated throughout the corridor.

Rhonda surveyed the room and immediately turned around. "Hey, this ain't my cell. Where's my stuff?"

The guard leaned her head in through a small opening in the door. Her face twisted into an ugly smile. "Have a nice day."

Rhonda raced up to the face of the cell and pounded her hand on the door. "Come back here. Where am I? Why am I here?"

Exasperated, Rhonda leaned back against the bars. Bending her legs at the knees, she slid down until her bottom reached the floor.

The new prison cell was a hollow cube of concrete with no windows. Rhonda soon realized she would have no idea how much time passed in here or even if it were night or day. But that realization soon gave way to another reality. The cell not only had no light but also no furniture. Just a toilet at the back corner of the wall, a small steel sink, and a concrete cot covered in a thin mattress. Rhonda sobbed. She reached up and placed a hand on the wall. It was smooth but cool.

Rhonda sobbed until the heaves erupting from her chest seized in her throat, causing her to cough violently. She sniffed and with the palms of her hands, she wiped away the tears soaking her cheeks. She needed to stay calm and remain focused.

Calm and focused. Those were two characteristics that Lisa reminded Rhonda to maintain and two traits she'd learned were essential to people held in solitary confinement. As a condition of her situation, she had been allowed a visit to the library after breakfast once every three weeks. During her sixth week at Lakin, she found a book on the psychological impacts of isolation and why people who are alone, either by choice or by force, suffer.

Rhonda learned that people who had little to no interaction with others became anxious, paranoid, prone to panic attacks, and more. Women, especially, suffered further effects including depression, mood changes, and hallucinations.

She laughed as she replayed the information from the book in her mind. She sounded like one of those quack psychologists who appeared on daytime talk shows where they sat and psychoanalyzed someone in one hour and spewed out a bunch of babble that most of the people in the audience and people watching at home didn't understand.

She fell asleep. Rhonda remembered waking up when a meal tray that was slid through a slot in the cell door. She began shouting at the guard through the open slot, demanding to know why she had been moved and when she would be moved again. The mental exhaustion overwhelmed her. She fell asleep again but was then jostled awake by the same guard who had pushed her in the cell to begin with.

"Come on. Get up!" the guard barked. "It's time to go."

Sleep-smeared, Rhonda stumbled as she sauntered down the unfamiliar corridor, led by two guards dragging her. They made a sharp turn down a smaller corridor that bisected the hallway. Rhonda could hear the high, piercing screams coming from a woman near the bend in the hallway.

As Rhonda tried blinking the sleep from her eyes, she was tossed into another cell. The piercing wailing she heard earlier had intensified and then stopped.

Rhonda drank in her new location. This solitary confinement cell was similar to the other one, but it had two beds jutting outward from an exterior wall.

Before Rhonda could ask the guards anything, they slammed the door behind her. Squinting through the light, an imposing figure—tall and broad with a big dimple on her giant chin, wide gray pinstripes adorning the orange prison suit, jumped out from the bed.

The woman wrapped her arms around Rhonda and buried her face in between the crevice of Rhonda's breasts, panting heavily.

"Thank, God. Thank, God. I can finally talk to someone." The dull, earthy voice was eerily calming despite the circumstances.

Regaining her composure and focus, Rhonda pushed the woman away from her.

The woman backpedaled and looked up, eyes wide with astonishment and fear. She appeared to be in her mid-thirties, but Rhonda couldn't be sure. In prison, everyone looked older.

"First, what's your name?"

The woman swallowed hard. "Maria. Maria Hartley."

"Okay, Maria. Why are we in this cell together?"

"I—I don't know," Maria said, pacing around the room and tossing her hands in the air. "I had a hearing today in Kanawha County. I violated a condition of my parole. I was arrested for buying heroin from an undercover deputy sheriff." Maria stopped pacing and whirled around to face Rhonda. "Please," she asked, holding up a hand, "don't judge me or give me a lecture. Not now." Before Rhonda could say anything, Maria cut her off. "Some old codger of a judge, someone named Duncan, sentenced me here. See, I got Hep C. He said he'd send me here to get treatment, told me I had *special needs*. Whatever that means."

Rhonda felt a sickening pang in her gut. Maria charged close to her again, pointing her finger at a sharp angle, jabbing the air as she spoke. "What's worse, my stupid attorney, Ken, just stood there and let it all go on. Did and said almost nothing. I shouldn't be here. The infirmary already told me they don't have the medicine to treat the Hep. I shouldn't be here! I should be somewhere getting treatment!"

The reality of the new situation hit Rhonda hard like an old secret that had finally been revealed. Rhonda motioned toward the bottom bunk bed.

"Let's sit down. We need to talk."

The Trip

Mark rapped his knuckles on the glass dividing the driver and passenger compartments of the limousine.

The partition retracted, echoing a slow hum until it had disappeared entirely into a narrow slit cut into the plastic frame encased with polished wood. As Mark leaned forward, he could make out Reed's long neck and square face, which were partly shadowed by the burnished copper glow of the late evening's slanted light cutting through the glass into the driver's cabin.

"Can I help, Mr. Vincent?"

Mark pushed his head through the opening and let out a breath. "I just wanted to say that the funeral home is ten blocks ahead on the left."

Reed smirked at Mark and nodded. "Thank you, sir, for the reminder."

Mark pressed his hands flat against the wooden frame and settled back into the seat. He closed his eyes and let out a long breath as the whirling noise of the retracting partition stopped. "I really need to get back to work."

"Mark, please," Karen said, sitting on the back bench seat. "Alex just lost Danielle. Now is hardly the time to be thinking about work."

The seat Karen sat in faced forward, so Mark was unable to avoid the hard look she gave him. The other three seats between them had been folded into the floor so the aft compartment of the limousine was comfortable, but the noticeable chill brought on by Karen's whiny quip made the space feel awkward and cramped.

Mark folded his arms. "This attitude about work has nothing to do with this funeral and everything to do with the trip we didn't take."

Karen stared down at her feet, encased in polished, black-heeled shoes, crossed and resting against the rear compartment floor of the long-wheelbase car. Karen, pert and trim with cropped brown hair and pursed lips, wore a dark and neatly pressed pantsuit, which drew out her normally sour expression. However, now her expression was weary.

"I did want to go to Hawaii a few months ago. I did." Her normally professional tone even sounded weary. "But I understand there was that big account that needed attention."

"More than just attention," Mark scoffed. "That was the biggest account our firm had signed in nearly ten years. Ten years. Think about that, Karen. The commission I made from that deal pays for our life." He held out his arms and swept them through the open space in the compartment. "Pays for this."

Karen nodded slowly. "I understand." She looked out through the tinted window and sighed. "The trip was about more than just going somewhere, Mark. It was about us getting a chance to be together. Spend time *together*."

"We see each other every day."

She leveled a hard look at him. "That's not what I mean. When we're here, there is always *something*. The phone rings, a client emails you, something that keeps us from ever truly being together. Just us."

Mark shook his head. "I think you're exaggerating. Those phone calls and emails allow us to live life in a manner that we deserve."

"I would want to be with you even without the money."

Mark let out an impish laugh. "Life would be very different for us without it."

Karen slid down slightly in her seat. "Money is not everything, though."

"Not always. But it sure makes life much easier."

Karen set her jaw and stared again out the darkened window. The downtown Columbus landscape whirled by as the limousine sped along. The asphalted downtown streets that were black during the day melted into the dusky skylight. When a car passed the limousine, its headlights reflected in the water puddled on the street after the rain earlier that day. The standing water and the darkness hid the back alleys, garbage dumpsters, parked cars, and the smell of petrol that were also part of the downtown Columbus landscape.

After Karen let the silence settle, she broke it with a biting realization. "All the money Alex and Danielle had didn't help Danielle in the end."

Mark sighed with his own resignation. "Honey, Alex is the best trial lawyer in Columbus. Heck, probably the best in Ohio. He's never lost a case, *ever*, in his entire career."

"I know—"

"Their money allowed Danielle to go to the cancer center at Duke University and work with some of the best hematologists in the country. If Alex were an ordinary laborer or a teacher or worked in some other more menial service job, they never would've been able to go to Duke. Those visits down there and the treatments they provided helped Danielle live a longer, better life. That is what money—earned the right and honest way—can offer."

Karen stopped listening. Mark always brimmed with opinions and anecdotes from a life lived to extremes as a hedge fund manager. That, combined with the impenetrable self-confidence he maintained, is what attracted Karen to him when they married ten years ago, but that trait also made it difficult to have conversations about serious issues that required some depth and perspective.

"I understand all of that," Karen replied after Mark had stopped speaking for several seconds. "I think Alex and Danielle would have traded all of their money and prestige and all of those professional accomplishments if it meant she could be cured of leukemia."

Mark arched an eyebrow at Karen and waved a finger at her. "The Alex Staton I know would've wanted that and the money that came with the work. Believe me."

As Karen prepared to escalate the discussion, the limousine slowed and lilted to the left.

Mark clapped his hands together. "Good. We're here." Mark removed the silver Tiffany cufflink from his white dress shirt and pushed back the sleeve. His gold-plated wristwatch ticked slowly under the fluorescent overhead lights.

"If we only stay for twenty minutes, I can have Reed take me back to the office so I can get another hour or two of work in." His face brightened. "I'm ready to close the new account with OhioHealth. It would bring another big account for our JPMorgan Chase office and provide me with another hefty commission."

"Mark, please."

He waved his hand past his face, dismissing her comment. "It will be fine. Twenty minutes is plenty of time for us to pay our respects. Besides, Alex knows *everybody*. By the end of the viewing, he won't even remember if we were here or not."

In a moment, Reed had opened the side door near the front of the compartment, and Mark slid himself across the leather seats on the bench.

"I expect you to be nice and kind and thoughtful and respectful," Karen commanded, causing Mark to stop and turn toward her. "I mean it. I don't want to be rushed. Don't push me along or around like you do when we are having dinner with your potential clients." Her tone was icy. She seemed to bite off the end of each word as she spoke. "I loved Danielle like a sister, and I love Alex, too. We are operating on their timetable, not ours."

Mark blinked once and swallowed hard. "Finished? Can we go inside the funeral home now?" There was a gleam in his eyes, almost like a dare.

Karen removed the small mirror from her evening purse and checked her reflection. After tightening and pursing her lips twice in some type of exercise, she smacked her lips shut and then pushed herself off the rear leather seat.

Reed offered Karen a hand and helped her out of the low-slung car into the orange glow of the streetlamps in downtown Columbus, which created a warming effect on her skin. Ahead, Mark had already climbed the three small steps to the front door. Light filtered through a gap in the two long curtains that accented the funeral home's entrance from the inside. As Karen looked up, she could see stars resembling pinpricks on the black canvas sky, but none of the light seemed to filter through the hazy night air to make any difference when she looked away.

As they entered through the front door of the funeral home and made their way down the corridor to the chapel, Karen felt her legs wobble. Grief tore at her as she noticed the wide entryway to the chapel at the end of the corridor. Tears fell thickly on her cheeks, and her voice stuck in her throat. There was still time to turn around and walk out, back onto the street and into the comfort and incognito existence the limousine provided. But she couldn't do that to Alex or Danielle. Especially Danielle.

Karen reminded herself that they were more than just casual visitors paying their respects. They were close friends of the deceased and her husband. Danielle had always been there for Karen.

When Karen suffered a miscarriage two years ago, Danielle came by the house almost daily for six months. Often, she would bring chicken salad sandwiches and sweet tea, Karen's favorite. Danielle and Alex had been unable to have children after a car accident left Danielle infertile when she was a teenager, but that experience and her lack of knowledge about pregnancy and childbirth didn't matter. Many times, Danielle would just sit quietly with Karen or listen as Karen shared her sadness, frustrations, and grief over losing the baby and the fact that Mark had blended back into his normal work routine effortlessly after only three days. Danielle never judged Karen or made any summations about her thoughts and feelings.

Now Karen had to do the same for Danielle and for Alex. In the days since Danielle died, Karen had wondered what it would be like for her if Mark died first. What was Alex feeling after seeing his wife, his high-school sweetheart, die from a horrible disease that wrecked her body and left him alone and bereft of the one person he loved more than anyone else in the world?

A warm hand pressed into the narrow space between her shoulders. Mark's warm press snapped Karen from the reverie, and she looked over at her husband. With his cleft chin, widow's peak, the black spill of wispy hair and rinsed blue eyes, he resembled the type of handsome man anyone might encounter in a romance novel or a business textbook about how to resemble someone in charge of all situations.

At the end of the hallway, an elegantly dressed man in a suit with high-planed cheeks and wide eyes greeted them then asked them to sign the register book and take a memorial folder. Mark quickly scribbled their names in the book, snatched two folders, and charged into the chapel.

Karen sheepishly trailed behind her husband. As Mark strode in before her, Karen was shocked to see the chapel was basically empty. The room was painted cream with two brown sofas running along each outer wall. A marble fireplace near the side of the room away from the casket was neatly adorned with a purple lace garter. Two side tables at the back of the room each held a lamp, which was turned on and shot an obtuse level of soft white light onto the ceiling. Wooden pews with padded seats ran the width of the room and served as a focal point in dividing the casket and the family from people entering the chapel.

"Mark, please. Slow down," Karen whispered.

Mark stopped and rested a clenched fist on his hip. With an inviting glance, he reached back and forcefully grabbed her arm, sliding it into the open space between his arm and side.

As Karen made an inaudible groan, Mark dropped his fist, pressing Karen's arm into his side.

Mark centered his eyes past Alex and onto the closed casket at the front of the chapel. "Look, honey. A bronze casket. Nice! That must have cost them seventeen-grand, easily."

"*Shhh*," Karen replied. "Alex is looking right at us."

"Allllexxxx," Mark said in an exaggerated playful tone.

Alex, with his thin frame, prominent cheekbones, sparkling green eyes, and pouty pink lips, grinned nervously, unsure of what to do or say.

He extended a shaky hand, and Mark grabbed it immediately and embraced his friend in a half hug. "Good to see you. I mean, considering the circumstances."

Karen kicked Mark's foot with the toe of her shoe, but Mark ignored the gesture and broke the embrace with Alex. As Karen settled a look on Alex, he hardly resembled the person she remembered.

When Alex moved after the hug with Mark, his whole body hung limp as if each limb weighed a ton and moving was a slow, painful effort. His irises were threaded scarlet, and his eyeballs hung heavy in their sockets. His gaze darted away from Mark and onto Karen.

"Oh, Alex. I'm so sorry." Karen stepped forward and offered a hug. Alex wrapped his arms around her in an embrace. Karen found herself squeezing tightly, transferring her thoughts and sadness into the strength of the hug.

"Thank you." His voice quaked. "And thank you for coming. Both of you. Danielle thought the world of the two of you. She and I were only kids, but she always said that if we'd had siblings, she would want them to be like you." Alex then looked away, his features stiff.

Karen cocked her head to the side and raised her shoulders. "How nice. We loved Danielle, too."

She cut a side-glance at Mark, who was busy taking inventory of the room. "So where is everybody?"

Alex lifted an eyebrow, and his mouth tilted. "The viewing just started a few minutes ago. You are the first ones here."

Karen reached a hand and placed it on Alex's arm. "What is it that we can do? Mark and I will do anything. Call anyone, go to the grocery store—"

Alex rubbed his chin and sighed. "I appreciate the offer, but I can't think of anything right now."

Karen patted his forearm. "It doesn't have to be anything for us to do right now. In the days ahead, I can only imagine things will come up that need attention. And I, or *we* want you to call on us. I mean that."

Karen stood up straight, feeling Mark eyeing her suspiciously from behind.

"Well, like Karen said, let us know if we can do anything."

Karen felt Mark grab her arm from behind, and she jerked it away. She stepped to the side of Alex and placed a hand on the casket for a moment, feeling the coolness of the bronze metal against her skin. Karen took in a deep breath and closed her eyes for a few seconds, honoring her friend Danielle with the touch and the silence.

Mark clapped his hands. "Okay. Well, we need to get going. Right, honey?"

She spun on her heel and scowled. "Just a few more minutes, please." Her voice was ice.

Mark squinted at her and shook his head, then leaned into Alex. Mark could smell an overpowering aroma of spice, sweetness, and floral coming from Alex's cologne.

"Don't pay any attention to her," Mark said, mockingly. "She's a little sore with me because we didn't take the trip to Hawaii a few months ago." Mark rolled his eyes.

Karen turned around and stepped closer. "Please, Mark. Not now. This is not the time. Or place."

"Nonsense. Alex is like family. It's okay if he hears about our little disagreement." He focused his gaze back on Alex. "I mean, Karen wanted to make it a big fight, but I wouldn't let that happen."

Karen fumed. She lunged forward and grabbed Mark by the tie. "Not here. Not now. Tonight isn't about us. It's about Alex and Danielle."

Mark held up both hands in a surrendering gesture. "Don't get all preachy with me because you didn't get what you wanted."

Karen watched Alex as his lips quivered and his eyes darted back and forth between them.

"Alex," Karen said, trying to get her anger under control and her voice stable. "I didn't see when the funeral is going to be. We would like to be here for that, too."

Stepping back, Alex widened his gait and gestured to the casket. "Danielle didn't want a funeral." He let out a nervous chuckle. "She didn't even want a viewing, but I had to convince her that it was an important process. It took some persuading, but I reminded her the viewing is for the living, for the people who loved her."

"That's absolutely right," Mark interjected, pointing a finger at Alex. "Funerals, viewings, they are always for the people left behind. I'm glad that Danielle finally saw it that way."

Alex dropped his gaze again, and his watery eyes shimmered in the low light. "I miss her so much."

"I know, of course," Karen said, turning back and hugging Alex. He wrapped his small hands around Karen and pulled her close.

Karen could hear Mark's breathing grow heavy as the embrace continued.

"All right. All right. We shouldn't be sad. Let's not remember Danielle this way. We need to remember her for the vivacious person she was when she was alive. I don't think she'd want us standing here all mopey and feeling sorry for ourselves."

Alex looked back at Mark and blinked away some tears. "You're right. She wouldn't."

Mark tilted his head and furrowed his brow. "Because I am never going to remember Danielle this way." He lifted his chin at the casket. "She's not there. Not in my heart and not in my memories."

Karen wiped away a large tear from her eye as she pushed away from Alex and turned back to Mark. "That's the first smart comment I've heard from you all evening."

Mark gave a curt nod. "I think we need to go now."

Karen blew a thin stream of air between her lips. "Mark—"

"Mark is right," Alex pronounced, stepping between them. "Danielle would want us to spend some time talking about happy events. I want to hear about the trip."

Mark made a face. "What trip?"

"The one we didn't take," Karen added dryly.

"Oh, that one. I'm really glad we didn't go because Karen's mother, Wilma, wanted to go. She always wants to travel until it's time to go. Then she complains the entire time we are gone and talks about how she can't wait until we get home. I've never seen anything like that."

Karen whipped a look over at Alex. "He's exaggerating."

Alex's flat expression turned into a jocular grin. "I know. Mark does that a lot."

"No, I am telling the truth about that."

Karen shook her head. "We'd planned to take a seven-day cruise to Oahu, Kauai, Maui, and the Big Island." Her face brightened. "We were going to explore the Kualoa Regional Park, learn an authentic hula dance, surf…it was going to be great."

Alex grew sadder the more Karen spoke of the trip. When she finished, Alex looked down at the floor. "It sounds nice."

"And expensive," Mark added. "Too much. For what that cruise was going to cost, we could've taken three separate vacations."

"Which we wouldn't do because my husband would rather work."

Mark locked his hands behind his head and winced. "Karen, are we *really* going to have this discussion again?"

Karen crossed her arms and hardened her stance. "You're the one who brought it up."

"Uh, actually, I did," Alex said.

Mark and Karen both swung their gazes at him.

As silence fell, another couple—a tall, barrel-chested man with a red-tinged toupee and a short, waifish woman hunched over a walker—entered the chapel.

Karen peered over at the couple and then glanced back at Mark, who was shifting his weight anxiously between his two feet.

"Speaking of money," Karen said, dropping her eyes to the breast pocket on Mark's suit jacket.

Mark caught her look and stumbled. "Oh, yeah." He reached into the coat pocket and removed a check. "This is from Karen and me. We wanted to give a donation to the American Cancer Society in Danielle's name. I made a note on the memo line that the money should go to leukemia research."

Alex stared at the folded check for a moment like it was a foreign object he'd never seen before.

"Thanks, but that's really not necessary."

"It is, and we are glad to do it," Mark said, pulling up Alex's limp arm and stuffing the check into his hand.

Mark rested his thumbs into the lapels of his suit. He could hear the heavy and slow footfalls of the older couple behind him as the padded rods of the walker dragged across the carpet.

"Other people are starting to come in." Mark leveled a look at Karen. "Let's go, honey."

Karen gave a sympathetic smile and went and patted Alex on the breast. "Mark and I are so sorry about Danielle."

Alex, his eyes watery, nodded silently.

As Karen turned to walk away, Alex cleared his throat.

"I'm not being honest about something."

Karen nearly ran into Mark when he stopped walking, turned around slowly, and said, "If it's about the money, then it doesn't have to be a donation for the cancer society. Make the donation in Danielle's name someplace else. We just thought—"

"It's not about the money, but I need to tell you something about Danielle."

Mark's brow furrowed, and Karen felt a sharp pain stabbing her in the breast, a moment of concern that caught her in the throat.

"I don't understand," Karen mumbled softly. "What is it?"

Alex walked slowly up the aisle, accidentally kicking the end leg of the chapel pew. He stuffed his hands in his pockets and took a deep breath. "Danielle didn't die from leukemia."

Karen looked over at Mark. In that instant, his skin became gray, and his mouth hung open with lips slightly parted. His eyes and mouth were frozen wide open in an expression of stunned surprise.

Karen felt the blood drain from her face, and her mouth and face fixed in an incredulous expression.

Alex held up a hand. "I know this comes as a shock, but let me explain."

Karen and Mark exchanged quick glances with each other, but neither of them said anything.

Alex stared straight ahead, eyeing the older couple who stood behind Mark and Karen. Even though he was staring straight at them, Alex appeared not to notice them at all.

"In the early days of her chemotherapy treatments, Danielle felt okay. She was able to eat, still had most of her strength, and was encouraged that she was able to live her normal life. In fact, doctor appointments were the only things that disrupted her normal routine."

Mark relaxed his expression of shock, but he still refused to look at Karen or take his eyes off Alex.

"She knew—we knew from the doctors that this feeling would not last. The doctors called it cancer fatigue. It can come on suddenly and doesn't really result from any activity or exertion that Danielle would have done. Rest and sleep wouldn't help her. The whole fatigue is less precise, less cause-and-effect. Danielle was aware the fatigue would happen—it was a matter of time. So I asked her if there was anything special she wanted to do before she felt bad. Before her energy was zapped by the chemotherapy."

Karen felt her tongue dry and thicken in her throat. "What did she say?"

Alex darted his eyes back and forth between his friends. "She wanted to go on a trip. To Maine. We had gone up there for a summer wedding five years ago, and she fell in love with the place. She loved the rocky shores, the isolation, and being able to pack a picnic basket and spend the entire day in the woods."

Mark's normally strong voice came out as a rasp. "How was the trip?"

"We didn't go."

Mark arched an eyebrow at Karen, who looked back at Alex.

"I had a big case to work on. I was trying to make partner. That would have been a huge accomplishment for me. My parents never wanted me to go law school, so to be able to prove to them and myself that I could make senior partner at Alden Law would've been amazing."

The energy and force in his voice soon went away. "We were investigating an alleged collective bargaining violation between the unionized employees at Ohio State and the administration. The union hired our firm to represent them." Turning his head, Alex broke his frozen stare and looked at Karen and Mark. "Ohio State controls so much of what goes on in Columbus. When I was asked to be the lead attorney on the case, I knew this could be the case that made my career. The union had a strong case. We could've won."

His shoulders hunched together as if retelling the story made him want to disappear inside himself.

"When I told Danielle about it, we had a fight in our upstairs bedroom. I wasn't sure how to tell her, and when I was getting ready for work one morning, she came upstairs and brought me coffee."

Sweat began to bead on his brow. Alex rested the back of his hand against his forehead. A pained expression washed over his face.

"I don't even remember how it came up. Danielle was really upset. Doing something special for her was my idea, and she accused me of being selfish for putting my job ahead of her and her health."

Karen didn't look at Mark, although she could feel a cold stare coming from him.

"Danielle stormed out of the room, trying to balance the coffee cup while shouting at me at the same time. When she got to the landing and started down the stairs, she tripped on the first step. She fell down the stairs headfirst. When she reached the bottom of the steps, her neck was broken."

Karen gasped and placed her fingers over her lips to hide the shock.

Mark coughed and nervously tugged at the knot on his tie. "Alex," he spoke, his voice low and tinged with sadness. "My gosh. I'm so sorry. Karen and I had no idea."

Fresh tears streamed down Alex's cheeks. "I live with the guilt every day, the thought that my desire to make partner came between my wife and me. I mean, who knows how many months we would've had left, but I didn't want—" His voice caught, and his words came out as a whimper. "But I didn't want to be the reason she died." As he began sobbing, Karen went over and placed her arm around him again. "That's why I can't accept the check. I don't deserve it, and I'm not sure Danielle would want me to have it anyway."

Alex held out the check, and Karen reluctantly took it.

"There is something the two of you can do that would mean more to me than money."

Karen walked over and handed the check to Mark, who stuck it in the flap pocket of his suit coat. They both looked back at Alex to find him wiping away his tears with a handkerchief.

"Take the trip."

"Excuse me?"

Mark looked perplexed. "To Maine?"

The question allowed Alex to let out a snort. "No. Take the trip to Hawaii. Do it. Don't worry about if the time is right, or if work can be avoided, just go. Be together. Remind each other why you fell in love and why you matter to each other. I would give anything, anything to take back the argument I had with Danielle and the decision I made to work instead of going on the trip with her." Alex strode forward, his face red, wet, and puffy. "Please, promise me."

Karen and Mark exchanged glances with one another before both looking over at Alex. "We promise," they said in unison.

For the first time, Alex smiled. "I'm glad to hear that. Danielle would be, too."

Alex extended a hand, and Karen and Mark each shook it.

"Thank you for coming," Alex said flippantly, and Karen realized he had directed the comments to the couple behind them."

Karen pointed to the door at the rear of the chapel. "Let's go, Mark."

Mark waited for Karen to stand beside him before he marched at a brisk pace back to the limousine.

Reed tipped his hat and nodded to Karen as she collapsed into the bench seat of the limo, sitting in the area where Mark sat earlier. Mark sprawled out on the back seat. With one finger inserted in his ear, he spoke loudly into his cell phone.

He caught a glimpse of Karen and winked.

"Who was that?" she asked as Mark ended the call.

"A travel agent. I wanted to find out how soon we could book a trip to Hawaii."

The Ten Pin

Brett released the bowling ball, and it slid at first, but the lane's friction overcame the skid. The angle of the ball, wide and sweeping toward the pins, created a more oblique impact. All ten pins fell down.

He chuckled. "Just because it doesn't involve passes, points, and assists, doesn't mean it's not a real game."

Justin put the pencil aside and folded up the score sheet. "It's easy to sit there and say that when you beat someone in three games by a total of two hundred and ten pins."

Brett grinned. "Growing up in a bowling alley does make a difference."

Brett paused and looked around the Hinton, West Virginia bowling alley, appropriately named The Ten Pin, which had been empty for most of the evening. The concrete block structure kept the inside of the building consistently cool. The interior of the bowling alley was split into two spaces. A ten-lane bowling alley with seating areas and scoring tables occupied one side of the building. The other end of the building housed outdated, barely functional coin-operated arcade games and a concession stand that served some of the best bratwursts in West Virginia. Brett enjoyed the bowling while Justin enjoyed the food and beer.

Falling back into the narrow seat, Justin crossed his arms. He cut Brett a sharp look. "I can't imagine spending my time as a kid in a bowling alley. Dad and I went to basketball games and took trips around the world for fun, and you grew up in a dank bowling alley." Justin pointed at the lanes. "Go ahead and roll so we can get this over with."

Brett gripped the ball with two middle fingers and inserted his thumb into the remaining hole.

Looking down the lane, he saw fresh streaks of oil glinting from the wood. Most of the oil was located on the inside of the lane, leaving him roughly eight to ten boards of dry lane to be used.

Brett lined his feet slightly to the left side of the lane. He pushed off his heel on the first step, and held the ball parallel to his right ankle on the second step. Without thinking, the forward momentum of his moving feet carried him right to the edge of the foul line. He bent his knees then brought the ball back through and released it. His arm carried outward onto the lane, not upward.

The ball grazed over the wood and traveled in a relatively straight path down the lane. Suddenly, it varied a few boards to the left. The fuchsia red ball swirled and swiveled as it zipped down the lane until it smashed into the pins at the end of the surface. The force of the collision made Brett blink then smile. The technique worked again—he had rolled another strike.

"Dang it!" Justin exclaimed.

Brett turned and saw Justin disgustedly shaking his head and scribbling numbers onto the score sheet. The white t-shirt sticking out of his plaid button-down shirt blew back and forth under the air coming from the exhaust vent on the ball return machine.

"That gives you a six hundred and seventy-two series. I've never seen anyone have more luck than you."

Wiping the sweat from his brow, Brett walked back to the scoring table and plopped down next to Justin. He slapped him on the back.

"It's genetics, not luck."

"Doesn't matter. This isn't a real game anyway."

Brett waved off his friend's words, too flushed with his momentary victory to play his part in the friendly quarrel they'd been having over the sport since the first time Brett had persuaded Justin to come to The Ten Pin after school. They were both twelve then, each still struggling to find his place in the jungle of middle school. For ten years, they'd been chaffing each other about the game. Ten—just like the pins.

But Brett's connection to The Ten Pin went back further, to the time before he started school when he watched through the window of the nursery while his mother, in her red and white league shirt, would glide up the polished lane and release the ball. His mother loved bowling, and she always brought Brett along with her. For a time, he fussed and fumed over having to go to The Ten Pin. Yet seeing the joy wash across her face each week, coupled with a personal fixation on watching the spinning ball smash into the white pins, made each trip an experience Brett didn't want to miss. Now a college senior, he loved bowling more than ever.

Brett nodded at Justin and cast another long look at the other end of the bowling alley. Even though Hinton offered very little regarding entertainment, it did have a bowling alley. At times, he liked the fact that Hinton was quiet with a laid-back and relaxed attitude and the fact that everyone was helpful, friendly, and neighborly. Brett met so many people over the years at The Ten Pin that he assumed everyone in the town of twenty-four hundred people had visited the bowling alley at some point.

The door leading to the children's nursery, which was once located beside the concession stand, had been removed and wood paneling replaced it. The expense of babysitting services for those who were mothers coupled with the lack of regular bowlers made the program obsolete by the time Brett entered middle school.

Justin reached for Brett's wrist. "Look, I'm sorry about what I said. I didn't mean it to come out the way it did."

"Don't," Brett barked. "I don't need that from you right now." Brett sighed and waived off the remark. "Actually, it's okay. Bowling here keeps her memory alive for me." He paused and turned sideways, facing Justin. "I spent every Tuesday and Wednesday morning here while Mom bowled on two different leagues. She came here to take her mind off Dad's drinking and to do something for herself—" His voice trailed off.

Brett reached into his jeans pocket and removed a small locket. The long-tarnished gold necklace, regal and solid, held the last two pristine pictures of his mother before breast cancer took her health and her life. Brett rolled the locket around in his hand, fighting back the tears that welled up in his eyes. After five years, her absence in his life was still a fresh wound in his heart.

Brett tenderly slid the locket back into the pocket.

A short silence fell between them, and then Brett saw Justin look away and clear his throat. "I know your mom would be pumped to see you bowling like she did."

Brett massaged the folds of skin under his eyes as a tear slid between fingers.

"Besides, if you hadn't come down here to get out of the house and me away from my mom when she was angry about something, we would have never done this together."

The comment struck Brett as slightly disingenuous. He flashed a sheepish grin at Justin.

"You have always hated coming down here and bowling."

"You're right. So I lied about that part, but I do enjoy any reason to hang out with you. The beer and brats are good, too. Speaking of which—"

Justin grabbed his wallet, tapped Brett on the knee with a clenched fist, and disappeared behind the lanes. Brett heard the metal glass doors open and slam shut farther down the bowling alley. A tall, muscular man wearing a sweatshirt with a hood approached Ruby at the front counter.

Ruby, a stout, pale-skinned woman, stood squarely upright and was a half step taller than the lithe, darker-skinned figure.

The alley, scented with the stale and acrid smell of cigarette smoke, was darkened by the jagged presence of the man and several shadows moving behind him. The tiny, front counter, shaped like an inverted horseshoe, dominated the center space as the small group huddled in clusters around it. The other stout shadows slipped away, heading for the snack stand, laughing and slapping each other on the backs and arms.

Ruby watched them move away from the counter and then leaned down. Brett watched her lips move as she reached below, found some bowling shoes, and pushed them across the counter. She looked down the bowling alley, located Brett and pointed at him.

Brett collected himself, wrung both hands together to evaporate the tears, and stood up as the figure grabbed the shoes and jogged to the lanes. A smile washed across his face. As the figure came into focus, the hood fell down. Logan had made it.

"Hey, man. I wasn't sure you'd come."

Logan stopped, bent over, and fumbled with his shoelaces. "I got lost. I had Mike give me a ride down here from the New River campus, except I couldn't exactly remember the directions." He swallowed large gulps of air as he spoke and kicked both shoes under the seats at the table. "How many games have you played?"

Brett turned away from Logan and looked at the scoring table. "Three, I think. Justin has been keeping score."

Logan teased his dark, bushy hair with two hands, trying to get the bands of hair that had been tossed to straighten. The hair matched his small, round, dark eyes and mocha-colored skin.

Across the bowling alley, a glass smashed into several pieces. The other guys laughed and shushed each other as Ruby raced over, pointing a finger at the group.

"You know those guys?" Brett asked Logan.

"One of them, unfortunately. I mean, fortunately. Heck, I don't know. The one guy is a classmate of mine at New River…

Chris something or other." Logan stopped and craned his neck. "I don't know who the other two are."

"Out of my way, man," Justin commanded as he nudged Logan, holding a tray level to his chest. "I got beers and brats here. It's the food of champions." Justin winked at Brett.

Brett looked at Logan, who laced his bowling shoes tightly to his feet by tying double knots.

Brett swallowed, and a knot formed in his stomach. He hadn't told Justin he had invited Logan to bowl with them, much less that Logan had accepted. Justin would be furious. Brett and Justin had been best friends since elementary school, and Justin always talked about how much he always wanted to spend time with Brett. For a while when they were teenagers, it was a great proposition. They had many classes together in high school, shared the same group of friends, and became as close as brothers, but college was different. Brett and Justin had drifted apart since their junior year at New River Community and Technical College, mainly because Justin hung out with a different group of friends. When Brett asked their names, Justin became evasive. Then Justin started arranging things for them to do on weekends but never showed up. Brett liked Logan ever since the two had lived in a residence hall together during their freshman year. When Logan casually mentioned that he would like to learn to bowl, Brett initiated the invitation to join him and Justin for their weekly Friday afternoon bowling.

Brett took a deep breath, searching Justin's face for a reaction. He then dropped his gaze to the floor before refocusing it on Justin.

"Can't you say excuse me?" Brett asked Justin, pointing at Logan as he spoke.

"I can, but I won't." Justin blinked and looked at Logan again. "Who exactly is this?"

Brett sighed. "Justin, this is Logan. Logan, Justin."

Logan smiled and extended his hand. "Nice to meet you, officially. We have class together on Monday mornings—"

Justin cut him off and said to Brett, "I should have asked if you wanted any beer and how much food you wanted. Getting my rear end kicked in bowling always makes me hungry."

Justin rested the tray gently on the seats. Some white, frothy foam had spilled over the side of the plastic cup and formed a small pool on the tray. Justin swiped it with his hands and rubbed them on his pants. He looked quickly at Logan and then leveled a look at Brett.

"What's he doing here?"

Brett felt the tightness in his stomach move to his throat. "I invited him. Logan likes to bowl, and I told him after class today you and I were coming down here to bowl, and he was welcome to join us." Brett waited for the response.

Justin scoffed. "I don't like people, especially ones I don't know."

Brett took a step closer to Justin. "I know."

A look of confusion washed over Logan as he crossed his arms. "Look, if I have come uninvited, I can leave."

Justin looked at Logan through the corners of his eyes, and his entire demeanor changed. He flashed a toothy smile and extended his arms outward. "Nah, I'm just joking. I'm glad you're here." Justin gave Logan's chest a faint bump and slapped him on the arm.

Logan nodded.

"Really, I'm just glad someone else is here to get destroyed by mister PBA himself over there."

Logan chuckled. Justin talked back to Brett as he moved away. "I need to learn how to play this stupid game."

Justin craned his neck, watching Logan fumble through the rack of balls. "What the heck is he talking about?"

"Never mind," Brett replied.

Brett had tried to explain the intricacies of bowling to Justin many times, but Justin ignored them. Instead, he wanted to stand in the middle of the lane, throw the ball straight, hard, and fast, and then he complained when he never earned strikes or chances to pick up spares. Actually, Justin liked to complain about it a lot, and the more beer he drank, the louder he complained. When Brett first talked about bowling to Logan, Brett appreciated Logan's interest in the techniques of the game and his desire to learn some of the bowling jargon.

The slow grind of the ball return machine screeched and then stopped. Brett looked back at the front counter as Ruby flipped two switches. Unsure of the situation, she turned off the lanes.

As Brett removed his wallet and pried open the slit at the top, Justin stepped closer.

"Justin, can you just step back from me for a second. You are starting to give me a complex."

Justin furrowed his brow and took a step back. Brett hated being so brusque with his friend, but the fact that Justin always had to be so close to him when they were together made Brett feel uncomfortable at times.

"Uh, I got this one," Justin replied. "How many more games are we bowling? Three more? We want to give Jake a chance to bowl."

Logan cleared his throat. "Um, it's Logan."

Justin rolled his eyes. "Whatever." Justin flipped through a stack of cash held together by a silver money clip.

Brett didn't intend to stare as Justin cracked the fresh bills by separating them with a thumb, but Brett managed to see several one-hundred-dollar bills turn over.

"That's a lot of cash to be carrying around."

Justin stopped turning the cash and held it. "It's just some walking around money. Dad gave it to me as an allowance."

Brett searched his mind, trying to remember what Justin could have done to deserve such a large amount of money.

Walking around Justin again, Logan stepped between them and rested the bowling ball inside the groove of the return machine.

Sitting down at the table, Brett wrote their names on the score sheet.

Justin slapped Brett on the back. "Why don't you losers start practicing, and I'll pay Ruby for three more games."

Logan seemed uncomfortable with the decision. He held some money in front of Justin. "Here. I've got some money to help pay."

Justin grabbed the hand and pushed it downward. "Don't worry about it. I've got it. The beer and brats are on me, too. Have as much as you want. I'll get more if we need it."

"But I'm under age. I can't really drink."

Justin flexed the muscles in his mouth tightly. "Please. Nobody is going to tell anybody. I'll be back."

Brett rested the pencil on the table, stood up, and approached the lanes. Logan stood behind him, talking softly as Brett extended an arm forward, then made a quick, slicing motion into the air several times.

When something else smashed against the floor across the bowling alley, Brett looked back. Ruby flung up her arms in disgust, then grabbed the broom and small dustpan behind the counter and stormed off across the alley. Brett made more diagonal motions in the air.

"What are you doing," Logan asked, now standing on the approach opposite Brett.

"Lining up a possible shot at the ten pin. I left several of them during the last game."

Logan crossed his arms. "So you flail your arms in the air and that helps?"

Brett cut Logan a sharp look and then grinned. "Nope. To pick up the ten pins, I have to make a slight movement either up or back on the approach. I try not to move more than six inches up. That helps me get the ball to the pocket more quickly, giving the ball less time to react, which creates more rotation. The trick is in your movements. If you get too close to the lanes on the approach, you can't see as well. If you stand too far away, then the movement on the ball is slowed. It all depends on how close you get."

"How well do you know Justin?"

The question struck Brett as slightly off topic. "He and I have been friends since forever. Why?"

"Nothing. It's just when we've talked and hung out, you've never mentioned being buddies with Justin."

Brett let out a small laugh. "Justin takes a while to warm up to. We have a long, sometimes complicated friendship. Anyway, I didn't need to bring him up, so I didn't—"

Logan cut him off. "We have a psychology class together. He sits near me because our professor puts us in assigned seats so she can take roll faster. He's never spoken to me before, but I see him talking to some guys after class a lot."

Brett thought about the talk he'd had with Logan earlier. "Is the guy's name Chris?"

Logan shrugged. "Might be. I think I've heard Justin address him by that name before."

Ruby let out a disgusted groan behind them as she returned to the counter.

"You think the lady might need some help?" Logan asked.

Brett let the question linger for a moment. He scanned the bowling alley and realized that nobody else was bowling. "Yeah, let's see if she needs our help and find out exactly what's going on."

Brett and Logan ascended the three narrow steps leading from the lane area to the main floor. As they crossed the bowling alley, they saw Ruby dumping large pieces of broken glass from a dustpan into a trashcan. Ahead, a mostly full pitcher of beer was soaking the carpet.

"Where's Justin?"

Ruby leaned over the bar. "I threw all of them out."

Brett looked at Ruby, narrowing his eyes. "Why? Justin was bowling with us."

Ruby leaned back. "Nope, those boys were drunk or stoned or something. They wanted some beer, and I told them no. They didn't like my answer." Ruby pointed to the drenched carpet. "Justin followed them outside."

Logan walked to the front door. "I don't see anything."

Brett strode to the door and shoved it open. The air, soft and hazy, melted into the rich, mellow sunlight sweeping across the mountains behind the parking lot. The bowling alley, crammed against a narrow embankment near the edge of the Route 3 highway, signaled the beginning of downtown Hinton, now growing quiet as dusk began.

Brett saw Justin talking to two men, both of whom seemed slightly older than Justin. One of the men had fair hair and a sharp chin with pale skin and blue eyes. He wore trim blue jeans, a black and green retro short-sleeved button-down shirt, and black boots.

He spoke first. "Who the heck are you?"

When Brett stopped walking, Logan did as well but broke his stride too late and nearly crashed into the back of Brett.

Brett squinted at the man for a moment. "Do I know you?"

The man's face grew tight, and his lips pressed flat. "I'm Deacon. I don't like a question answered with a question."

Brett squared his shoulders. "I don't really care," he said, cutting a sidelong glance at Justin. "Justin, what's going on?"

Logan tapped Brett on the shoulder. "I don't think we should mess with these guys."

The second guy, broad-shouldered and barrel-chested with sapphire eyes and crimson lips, grimaced and clenched his fists. He was bigger than all of the guys in the parking lot and outweighed everyone by at least twenty-five pounds. His gray sweatshirt and jeans hugged his taut frame.

Deacon and his friend could sense the tension. "Easy, Kyle."

Nobody moved. Brett could hear his own heartbeat. He could even hear nervous breaths coming from Logan.

Brett noticed Justin trembled slightly. Sweat formed on his face, and Justin wiped his face on his shirt.

Deacon looked back at Justin and then nodded over to Kyle. "We need to talk to Justin about something." A gleam flashed in his eye that made Brett even more anxious. "We are going to take him for a little ride. I promise we will bring him back."

"In one piece, too," Kyle added. The dulcet tone of his voice masked its raspy quality. Kyle grinned, but nobody found the joke funny.

Justin had avoided looking at Brett, but he finally slowly looked over at his friend. The twitch in Justin's eyes signaled something to Brett, but he didn't know what it meant.

Parked behind Deacon and Kyle was an orange Jeep Wrangler. Holding his position in the parking lot, Deacon reached back and flung open the door. He snapped a finger, and Kyle came over, patting Justin on the back and pointing inside the car. Justin froze for a moment before finally loosening his posture and moving to the car.

Brett stepped forward, and Logan grabbed his arm. "Don't, Brett," he whispered. "One of them has a gun."

Brett watched Kyle and Deacon intently. He squinted through the low-hanging sunlight and could make out the handle of a gun jutting up from a holster clipped to the back of Kyle's belt.

Brett looked back at Logan. "We have to do something. Justin is in trouble."

Almost as if Justin had heard Brett, he called back from the Jeep. "I'll be fine, Brett. I just need a little bit of time to clear things up. I'll be back later."

With that, Kyle pushed Justin into the back seat as Deacon moved around the front of Jeep. As the doors thumped shut, Ruby came stomping out the front door.

"Those the guys who made a mess inside?"

Brett and Logan didn't turn around but instead looked ahead. Deacon dropped down the clutch and lurched the car forward before slamming on the brakes. The Jeep began skidding. The hard braking caused the rubber tires to slide laterally on the parking lot with a dull squeal that sent smoke pouring out from under the cab.

As the smoke curled and wafted in the air, Deacon threw the clutch again and hit the gas. The Jeep lurched forward again, this time rocking slightly to the right before balancing and turning the corner onto Route 3.

"Bunch of brats," Ruby scoffed, wiping her hands off. "There's got to be a few hundred dollars of damage inside. Broken glass and chairs. A real mess."

Brett and Logan slowly looked back at Ruby. She searched their faces, and her eyes grew wide, drawing out the wrinkles and grooves in the corners. "Oh, no! What's happened?"

Inside The Ten Pin, they helped Ruby clean up the broken glass near the snack bar and beside the counter. "All I said to them is that they had to pay *before* they could bowl and that I was not going to tell them anything about Justin. If they wanted to talk to him, he was here." Ruby brushed the last granules of broken glass into the dustpan and emptied them into the trashcan. "When I told them that, they went berserk and started tearing up the place."

Brett had spent the last several minutes telling Ruby what happened. "Tell me all of it and don't leave out one single detail," she had demanded. Brett had even told her his suspicions and fears. While Logan remained mostly silent, Ruby didn't seem too concerned.

"We all know Justin. He's spoiled and he's lived fast and loose most of his life. That's the problem coming from a single parent home where the father has to work the whole time, and the kid doesn't know his daddy. He learns to raise himself and be with people who fill a need. I wouldn't worry too much."

Ruby's comments didn't make Brett feel any better. Another couple had come into the bowling alley as Brett and Logan finished putting the broken arms of the chair into the trashcan.

Even though Brett and Logan decided to bowl a few more games and wait for Justin in case Deacon and Kyle brought him back to the bowling alley, Brett wasn't in the mood to bowl. So he spent little time ensuring his fingers were inside the ball correctly or that he was lining up his shots according to the painted arrow placements on the lanes. Instead, he basically went up to the lane on each turn and threw the ball right down the middle, not even watching to see where the ball landed as it clacked against the pins.

Logan took his turns more seriously and tried teasing and taunting Brett as the games went on. Brett managed a few grins and smiles but remained mostly silent.

At the end of the second game, Brett looked at the clock on the far wall, its surface stained yellow from years of cigarette smoke. "It's nearly six," he said, tossing a pleading look back at Logan, "and we still haven't seen or heard from Justin."

Logan nodded at Brett's cell phone sitting on the scoring table. "Try his cell phone."

Logan watched eagerly as Brett pushed the numbers and cradled the phone near his ear. After a few seconds, Brett shook his head and ended the call. "It went straight to voicemail."

With long strides, Brett walked away from the lanes. Ruby watched him pass by the counter. Brett felt like he should say something to her, but nothing came to mind. Brett could hear the lighter, faster footfalls of Logan behind him.

"Brett—"

"What?" he called back gruffly as he shoved open the front doors and skipped down the front steps into the parking lot.

Logan put a hand on Brett's shoulder. The sensation made Brett pull away. "What are you doing, Logan?"

"No, what are *you* doing?"

The hard edge in his voice made Brett stop. Brett shifted his eyes from the concrete lot and stared up, trying to recalibrate his thoughts. The low-hanging clouds that bracketed the sunset were laced with rust red. The light painted a rosy color on the trees that surrounded The Ten Pin. Brett loved fall in Hinton.

Soon, the mountains would be aflame in a riot of gold and red. Each leaf would dislodge from its tree and pirouette down to the earth as winter approached over the landscape.

Brett spun on a heel and leveled a look at Logan. "I don't know what to think or do, Logan. I'm really worried about Justin."

"I know what we can do." Logan fumbled with his cell phone in his pocket. "I'm calling the police."

Brett took a long stride forward and knocked the phone from his hand. Logan watched helplessly as the phone bounced off the concrete and caromed away from their feet.

"We can't call the police."

"Why not?"

"Justin would be so pissed at us if we did that."

"Who cares? Justin was basically taken at gunpoint, and we have no idea where he is or what's happened to him."

Brett sucked some air through his teeth. "Justin has been arrested before."

Brett could tell the revelation hit Logan in the pit of his stomach. Logan flapped his lips, trying to form a response.

"Assault. DUIs. He had a friend who knew one of the judges in town. The judge got him off and made the arrests go away on his record, so the Hinton police don't really like him."

Logan made a face and shook his head. "It doesn't matter. What's more important? Finding Justin or making sure the police like him?"

"I have a better idea," Brett said. "We will go look for him."

Logan crossed his arms and tapped his foot nervously. "If we do that, we make ourselves a target. Deacon and Kyle might come after *us*."

Brett arched an eyebrow. "Any better ideas because, shoot, I'm ready to hear them."

A cold, early evening wind blew between them, flapping a strand of Logan's hair near his face. A cold chill cut into Brett.

"Okay. Fine. We will take my car," Logan said and bent down to pick up his cell phone. "But where do we start looking?"

"I'll tell you. You drive."

The inside of Logan's faded green Geo Metro forced Brett to rest his chin on his bent knees in the passenger's seat. They decided to go downtown Hinton on Temple Street and see if they could spot the orange Jeep Wrangler parked anywhere. If Deacon and Kyle had made a mistake so far, Brett knew this was it. A large, brand-new car that shade of orange would catch the attention of people downtown, especially people coming home from work.

The engine of the Metro groaned and wheezed as Logan shifted between the brake and gas pedals. Brett told him to pull in front of the library and then slowly creep by the Hub Clothing Company. The shadows downtown lengthened as the evening sun touched the mountaintops. The store windows glowed orange from the sun's rays, but the shadows of patrons did not appear inside the shops. No cars were moving downtown, and few pedestrians loitered on the streets.

Logan pulled the car to the right side of the street in front of the Russell Stover candy store and threw the car into park.

"This is stupid," Logan whined. "These punks wouldn't take Justin to a place where they will be seen."

Brett looked out the window, thinking about how good a piece of chocolate would taste right now if the bile churning in his stomach from anxiety and desperation weren't making him nauseous.

"They might, especially if they wanted to talk to him. Taking him to the middle of nowhere looks like a kidnapping. Having a talk with Justin in a public place looks like a conversation and nothing more."

Logan let out a sinister laugh. "Do you really think that Kyle dude brought a gun to The Ten Pin and shoved Justin inside that car just to *talk* to him?"

Brett grew impatient. "Okay then, Mr. NCIS. Where should we look?"

Logan thought for a moment. "I think we call The Ten Pin and ask Ruby if she's seen Justin or the other two since we left. If not, we keep going on Route 20 and drive out to the woods near the high school. We should check everywhere, not just the obvious places."

Exhausted and overcome with frayed nerves, Brett reluctantly agreed.

They sped through downtown and merged onto Route 20 where Temple Street bisected Fourth Avenue. The neighborhoods outside of downtown were quiet. The slower pace of life in Hinton gave the place its charm, but Brett new that many emotions bubbled beneath the surface. Attitudes and feelings about everything ran deep in small towns like Hinton because everything was personal.

Brett felt guilty for sharing Justin's secret about being arrested with Logan, but since Logan was now part of the search, Brett wanted him to know the context of the situation.

The Metro thrummed as they came up the first hill on Route 20 just outside town. Brett used his cell phone and called The Ten Pin and spoke to Ruby. The call became garbled and ended before Brett could ask Ruby too many questions, although he was able to learn that she hadn't seen Justin, the Jeep, or Deacon and Kyle.

As they crested over the embankment, they saw a terrible scene. Cutting through the dusk, the coruscating lights of police cars and an ambulance pulsed like red eyes. A police officer, clad in an orange vest, held up a hand, motioning for them to stop.

Brett reached over and slapped Logan on the shoulder. "Slow down! Slow down, Logan!"

"I see it. I see it," he announced, slowly bringing the Metro to a stop about twenty yards away from the cop.

In front of them was a horrific scene. The pumpkin-orange Jeep Wrangler lay on its side with the metal on the hood and doors crushed like empty soda cans. Shards of glass were strewn all over the road. Through the windshield of the Metro, Brett could see Deacon's head leaning against the steering wheel, blood streaming down the side of his head. In front of the windshield, a white sheet had been pulled over a body.

"Holy cow," Logan mumbled.

Brett sucked in the cramped air, feeling his lungs caving in on themselves. He tried to speak, but nothing came out. Brett imagined Justin, lying on the cold asphalt of Route 20, the horrible pain he would have experienced as the crunching of metal and the tinkling of crushed glass numbed his hearing and pierced his skin, followed by the distinct cracking of his bones as he was tossed like a wet rag from the vehicle.

Brett shook with sadness and worry. A state trooper, clad in his stately green uniform, whispered something to the paramedic. Brett watched as the paramedic pointed to the body under the white sheet.

The state trooper nodded and then walked over to the deceased victim. When the paramedic crouched down and pulled back the sheet, Brett craned his neck to see who was underneath.

Logan followed Brett's stare. When the sheet was pulled back, Brett felt the muscles in his chest clench. He could make out the shirttail of the plaid button-down Justin had been wearing inside of the bowling alley.

Logan cut a look at Brett and then back to the crash scene. He frantically tapped a finger against the glass.

"Is that his body? Is that him?"

Brett swallowed hard and looked down slowly. "Yeah. Justin was wearing that shirt inside The Ten Pin earlier."

The pace of Logan's breathing quickened and he heaved. "Oh, my gosh. Crap! I'm going to puke."

Logan flung open the door, bent down at the waist, and let out a low groan as the sounds of a thick liquid hit the road.

Brett looked away and put his fingers in his ears, trying not to hear the sounds coming from Logan so he would not be tempted to vomit as well.

"We need to leave," Logan said, wiping a stream of spit away from his lips with his hand.

Brett looked at him with shock and fury. "No, we can't. We need to tell the police everything we know."

"No, not now," Logan said, plopping down inside the car and shifting the gearshift into reverse. "I need to go. I need to call my parents. I need to do something else." Logan's hands trembled as he wrapped his long fingers around the steering wheel. Sweat began to moisten his lip.

Brett put his hand on the gearshift. Logan's skin felt cold and clammy.

"No, Logan. The police will need to know what happened."

Logan whipped the car at an angle in the opposite lane. The policeman in the orange vest tossed a look down the lane as Route 20 disappeared around a bend into the woods. Satisfied, he waved a hand at Logan, indicating it was safe to drive ahead.

Logan stomped the gas pedal, and the car lunged forward. When the shadows of the storefronts in downtown Hinton jutted up into the sky like thick blocks of darkness, Logan pulled the car off to the side of the road and slammed the gear into park.

Before Brett could collect himself, Logan turned sideways in the seat and pointed his finger at Brett.

"The two of us don't know what happened other than what we saw at The Ten Pin. If we volunteer information now, it might make us seem suspicious. I know the cops will retrace where everyone has been today, and that is going to lead all of them back to the bowling alley at some point. We will talk to the police then but not before."

Brett puffed out a breath, a mixture between a laugh and a snort. "Logan—"

"Shut up, Brett. Given what you told me about Justin earlier and his run-ins with the police and this being a small town, we don't want to get swept up into something and be guilty by association."

Brett looked again out the window. The thick trees full of burnt orange and red leaves waved under an early evening breeze, almost as if they agreed with everything Logan had said.

Logan slammed his hand on the steering wheel. "I wish I had never come to The Ten Pin today."

Before Brett could say anything else, the trill of a cell phone hummed in the tight car cabin. Brett slowly swiped his finger across the screen, not even checking the number.

"Hello," he said, his voice a croak.

His eyes widened, and he slapped Logan several times on the arm. "Justin! Holy crap. Where are you? Logan and I drove out to Route 20 and saw—"

Brett abruptly stopped talking and nodded several times. "The Ten Pin. Okay, we will be right there."

"Justin's alive," Brett said breathlessly, swallowing several gulps of air. "He's back at The Ten Pin. Drive."

When they pulled into the parking lot, Brett nearly leaped out of the car before Logan had a chance to park. They both raced up the steps and burst through the door. Past the main counter, they found a solemn-faced and disheveled Ruby pointing to a table.

As Brett looked down, he barely recognized Justin. The color of his face was more purple than alabaster. His left eye was swollen, and his face was stained with congealed blood around the cheeks and chin. His shirt was missing and his jeans were dirty. Justin tried to say something, but the syllables didn't come out right, his cracked lips failing at the first attempt.

Brett dropped to one knee in front of Justin while Logan stood alongside Brett. Justin sat, staring at the floor, his lips trembling.

"Justin! What happened?" Brett peered up at Logan. "We just came back from Route 20, and we saw the wrecked Jeep."

Justin finally looked up, his eyed red-rimmed and moist. "I know. They're all dead."

Brett leaned back. "What? How do you know that?"

"Look," Logan cut in. "I don't know the two of you that well, but it's time to stop being so secretive about everything, and tell us what happened. All of it!"

Justin held a distant stare for a few seconds before biting down on his cracked lip.

"Those guys, Deacon and Kyle, I owed them some money."

Brett made a face. "For what?"

"I got in over my head gambling at the racetrack near Charleston. I owed this bookie named Chris a lot of money, and Deacon and Kyle helped me out."

Brett and Logan exchanged glances.

"I just about had everything caught up, and I went down there last weekend, had a few drinks, and the next thing I know, I was back into it with Chris for five grand."

"Dang, Justin," Brett said, his voice a mix of surprise and bemusement.

"This time, Deacon and Kyle wouldn't help me. I tried to go quiet for a while, but Chris sent Deacon and Kyle after me to collect the debt."

Logan let out a whistle. "Man, you are screwed, and you're an idiot."

Brett shot Logan a disapproving glare.

"What happened out on Route 20?"

The faraway stare in Justin's eyes returned. A shiver ran through his body. "Deacon and Kyle had never been to Hinton, and they wanted to take me someplace to rough me up. I didn't offer any places to go, so they drove through town until we got out onto Route 20. I saw Kyle pull out the gun, and that... that's when I knew they were going to kill me."

Ruby stepped into the space and offered Justin a bag of ice wrapped in a rag. He cautiously accepted it and rested it against his eye.

"I told them I had to take a crap."

"What?" Logan asked incredulously.

Justin was defensive. "It was the only thing I could think of to get them to stop and pull over. I told them if they didn't pull over, I was going to go all over the backseat. They argued for a bit and pulled over. When they did, Kyle told me to take off my shirt. Said he liked it and it would count against my debt. So I gave it to him. When I got back inside the car, Deacon said he found a clearing up ahead, and that's where we'd go. As we started to drive, I took my foot and kicked the gearshift on the Jeep. It shifted into park, and the car began to spin. Deacon tried to control it, but the car began to roll."

"I had my seat belt on, but the other two didn't."

Brett absorbed the story and recalled what they had seen. It was Kyle's, not Justin's, body under the white sheet.

"Everything went black. I must have been knocked out, but I don't for how long. When I woke up, I kicked out one of the back windows and crawled out onto the highway. I walked back to towards town for a while. Luckily, a highway department van was coming by, and he brought me here and called the police."

Brett and Logan knelt in front of Justin, and Brett took Justin's hand. "I'm just glad you're okay."

"Yeah, me too," Justin replied. He looked over at Logan, who looked guilty.

"Sorry for what I said earlier about not telling the whole story."

Justin nodded. "Forget about it. It's over now."

Ruby coughed a loud, throaty cough behind them. It was the type of cough meant to get the attention of someone else, not clear her throat of anything.

"I hate to break this meeting up, but there is a man here to see Justin. Says he knows you from the racetrack in Charleston." Ruby arched an eyebrow. "Justin, the guy said something about needing to get some bills settled with you."

Sexting

Harvey knew this moment was coming.

Through just over seven innings, Brian Clark of the Chillicothe Paints had given up two hits, and only one Butler Bluesox hitter had advanced past second base. Brian had struck out nine hitters, but that still wasn't enough.

Harvey looked through his binoculars at the meeting on the pitcher's mound.

"Yep. Hanning is just trying to see how Clark is feeling," Harvey mumbled. Nobody was sitting in any of the seats around him behind home plate, so the comments faded into the open space. Veterans Administration Memorial Stadium smelled of grass, dirt, and sweat.

"This team wins with pitching and defense," Harvey said again, pulling the binoculars from his face and holding them away from his chest. "If the pitching isn't there, we don't win."

Manager George Hanning motioned for the other players on the infield to join him on the pitcher's mound. Hanning lowered his head and kicked some tufts of dirt back and forth with his cleat. Brian stared straight ahead, facing home plate, shrugged his shoulders, and remained silent as the manager spoke.

A tight voice from the aisle interrupted Harvey's viewing. "Hanning always watches the pitchers too tightly."

Harvey turned to see Amanda standing in the narrow, cramped aisle. She cradled two hotdogs, wrapped like fragile babies in opaque plastic, against her chest and held a beer in one hand. The frothy foam on the ridge of the cup had bubbled up and over the plastic lip, settling in between her fingers.

Harvey peered up and took the beer from his wife. "That's true, but it's time to bring in Sonny Davis to shut things down."

Amanda rolled her eyes. "Brian Clark never gets enough credit—from you or anyone else."

She steadied the hot dogs in her hands and flopped down in the seat, pressing her feet against the seat in front of her. Amanda tore into the hot dog wrapper as if it contained a golden ticket.

Harvey turned his attention back to the pitcher's mound. The sun-drenched sky proceeded to bypass the stadium and slip behind the thick trees behind the center field wall. All afternoon, the sun lit up the sky in magnificent splendor. The rays beamed across Chillicothe for the entire day, and the sun represented an orange appetizer for the main course of crystal-clear blue skies with a touch of light breeze.

The narrow aisles were littered with empty food wrappers, plastic cups, and other refuse left behind from fans who had either left thinking the game was over or had consumed their fill of beer and hot dogs and decided to go somewhere else for entertainment. *Fair weather fans.* Harvey despised them.

"Look," Amanda said between small bites of hot dog. "I think George is going to keep Brian in there."

Harvey looked back to the mound. Brian Clark cut a sidelong glance at the Paints' third baseman, and his small, heady eyes darted between the rest of his teammates and the manager. Brian's mouth tightened, and he removed his cap, wiping the sweat from his brow with the back of his hand.

Amanda leaned into Harvey but kept her eyes focused on the field. "Brian can get the next batter out."

"I doubt it," Harvey quipped. "Clark might be able to muster enough strength to smoke another pitch or two past the ninth hitter in the Butler lineup, but if the batter reaches the base, the lineup will rotate back to the number one position. Dan Taylor hits first, and he led the summer collegiate Prospect League in stolen bases. There's no way after ninety pitchers that Clark will be able to get Taylor out."

Harvey looked over and regarded Amanda for a moment with her long, dark hair sprouting out from the Chillicothe Paints ball cap, her bright green eyes and her smooth skin revealing dimples at the folds in her cheeks. She had an athlete's build and small, supple breasts.

Her eyes were focused on the pitcher's mound, lips tight with her whole expression momentarily stoic.

"Brian is done, Amanda. His curveball is hanging in the zone much too high, and his fastball is losing velocity with each pitch. He's a two-trick pony. Once those pitches go, he's got nothing else."

The infielders nodded at each other and gave Brian a pat on the back. George Hanning stepped back, regarded the players, and then spun around and sauntered back to the dugout.

Harvey sighed. The decision was made. "Clark had better not make Hanning regret this."

Brian Clark took the stretch on the mound and fired the baseball to home plate. The movement on the pitch was high and inside, and Dan Taylor swung, sending the ball high into the air behind home plate. Nathan Turner, the catcher for the Paints, tossed off the catcher's mask and held his glove above his head, shielding the sunlight and squeezing his glove just as the baseball landed in its heel. Brian Carter had orchestrated the second out of the inning.

"Told you so." Amanda lovingly leaned into Harvey and placed her long, slender fingers on his knee. "I'm always right about these things."

They had been in residency together at Ohio State Wexner Medical Center in Columbus. Harvey had been attracted to the infused warmth that radiated from her amber skin any time there was a tense moment at the hospital. Amanda had an innate ability to steady a room, soothe a nervous patient or family member, and quell her own personal frustrations and fears about being a novice surgeon no matter the situation or circumstances.

It took Harvey a long time to muster enough courage to ask Amanda on a date. The first time he asked her, it was close to Valentine's Day, and they had been working in the emergency room at the hospital that week. After a difficult week of dealing with level one trauma emergencies, including victims of car accidents, gunshots, and drug overdoses, Harvey had a moment of courage and clarity that bubbled up under the fatigue and exhaustion that roiled him. Amanda said yes in an exasperated voice, which she insisted later wasn't intentional. After the first date, they connected on an emotional and sexual level that scared Harvey at first, but Amanda proved to be the same as a girlfriend as the person he'd observed in the hospital—warm and whip-smart.

Amanda had grown up in Cobb County, Georgia, just outside of Atlanta. Her father was a cop in Atlanta, and her mother worked as a nurse at Emory Hospital, so Amanda spent a lot of time in Atlanta. She often talked about the great shopping and restaurants Atlanta had to offer, but she also loved the opportunities to get outside the city and onto the great hiking trails that dotted the periphery of town to shoot the "Hooch," which meant tubing, kayaking, and canoeing trips on the Chattahoochee River. Her father loved baseball and would often take her to Fulton County Stadium and Turner Field to watch baseball with him when he was assigned security detail with the department.

Harvey had grown up in Chillicothe. He often told people it was a great example of Appalachian Ohio for better or for worse. Chillicothe had been a quiet and friendly place where everything in town was tucked close together, and everyone knew everyone else. Harvey felt safe growing up there, and he spent many summer nights listening to the Cincinnati Reds on his grandfather's old transistor radio.

But like most of central and southern Ohio, drugs and crime gripped the city. With that, many of the old Chillicothe families had moved away. Many of the good-paying jobs at the Kenworth and Mead plants were gone, and all that was left for work were fast-food restaurants or jobs at Kroger or Walmart.

Still, it was home for Harvey, and he liked working at the Adena Regional Medical Center and giving back to his community. Working at the same hospital as Amanda was also a benefit.

Harvey and Amanda had held season tickets to the Chillicothe Paints for several years. It was a chance for both of them to spend time together away from work and home responsibilities and enjoy the outside, which Amanda loved so much. The Paints' season began in late May and was over in early August, so the price and commitment weren't too great.

George Hanning stopped before exiting the dugout. He spun around awkwardly on a heel and stood on the second step of the dugout, then rested an arm on the railing. His body was robust and burly, replete with a fat gut hardly associated with a man who spent ten years as the first baseman for the Chicago Cubs in the 1990s and was a career .287-hitter. He retired from the game after being hit by a pitch in the face during the second game of a doubleheader against the St. Louis Cardinals in Chicago, an injury that permanently damaged the vision in his eye.

Harvey sucked in a breath. "Let's hope Hanning is right about Carter. Otherwise, this game is over."

Amanda looked over at Harvey for a moment, her gaze shifting to a space behind Harvey. As Harvey's eyes followed the stare, he felt a nudge on the shoulder.

A woman spoke. Her voice was flat, precise, and hoarse. "I don't think it's necessary for us to sit right behind home plate, Trent."

"I like sitting behind home plate, Regina," a gruff voice cracked back. "I can really see if Brian's getting it to the plate."

As Brian moved to the height of the mound, Trent and Regina slid into the row in front of Harvey, blocking the view of home plate. Amanda leaned far to the right and cupped both hands over her eyes to see. Harvey made a face and craned his neck in between the open spaces of the passing couple, trying to see.

"Strike," the umpire called out. That was followed by the slap of the ball hitting Brian's glove back on the pitcher's mound as the catcher tossed it back.

"Who's at the plate?" Harvey asked Amanda, still trying to see the field. "I can't see."

"It's Micah Camerillo."

"Aw, crap."

The couple in front of them settled into their seats. This time, the man's beefy shoulder blocked the view of the field. He turned around, a sly grin crossing his face.

"Easy now," he said in a slow drawl, spitting tobacco juice in a cup. "That's my boy out there on the mound."

Harvey paled, and he felt Amanda jab him with a sharp elbow to the ribs.

The man spat again into the cup, and the woman next to him flung a napkin in his direction, not taking her eyes off the field.

"Oh, well, it's nice to meet you." Amanda glared over at the man, and Harvey shrugged his shoulders, unsure of what to say to break the uncomfortable moment that passed between them.

The man turned his head to the side and called back. "Name's Trent. This is my wife, Regina."

"I'm Amanda, and this is my husband, Harvey. Great to meet you," Amanda chirped, slipping an open hand in between them. Trent ignored the gesture while Regina looked down at the hand, a puzzled look in her eyes. Her skin was as weathered as a crocodile handbag. She wore a spaghetti-strapped cream-colored top with an opening in the back, which revealed strong muscles between the shoulder blades.

Regina limply took Amanda's fingers and wiggled them. "Good to know ya."

Trent clapped his hands and leaned forward. "Come on, son. Get this sucker out," he barked.

Amanda and Harvey exchanged glances. "Come on, Brian!" she called out.

Harvey leaned into her, his voice a sharp whisper. "What are you doing?"

She looked back at him, perplexed. "Cheering for the Paints."

Harvey rolled his eyes and sat back in his seat.

Nathan Turner, the catcher for the Paints, raked his left hand on his inner thigh, signaling for a curveball. Brian nodded and covered his lips and chin with the face of the glove. Brian leaned back and fired the ball to the plate. It landed low and outside. Micah Camerillo jumped back from home plate to avoid being hit by the pitch.

"That's all right," Trent hollered out, his baritone voice and words coated in nicotine erupting throughout the ballpark. "That's just ball one."

Harvey, with his hands pushing on the handrails, pressed up from the seat to sit higher.

Brian got the sign again from Nathan. Micah Camerillo dragged the barrel of the bat against the ground and raised it over his shoulder. Brian spun a beautiful curveball, but this time, the pitch landed low and inside, and Micah watched harmlessly as it nearly bounced in front of home plate.

Frustrated, Nathan shook his head and looked to George Hanning in the dugout for another option.

In the seats behind home plate, Harvey steepled his hands and blew air through the space in his fingers. "Fastballs. He needs to throw a fastball. Call for one, Hanning. Signal to Turner to call for that pitch."

Trent slowly turned around in his seat until he was perched on its edge and locked eyes with Harvey. His droopy face and the fleshy bags under his sockets stuck out under his thoughtful, hooded eyes. Trent could feel Regina and Amanda following his glare.

"I thought my boy was done," Trent said, more as an accusation instead of a statement. Trent tilted his head upward as if he were trying to recall a memory. "I think something was said about my boy not having enough strength and energy to get through it."

Harvey's eyes widened, and Amanda placed a hand back on his knee while Regina Clark held an uneasy stare.

"How did you hear me say that?"

Amanda butted in. "That's not really the point."

Harvey cut a look over at his wife to see her tilting her head slowly to the side and pursing her lips.

"It's not," Harvey said, sputtering. "I just meant, well… I've watched Brian pitch for a long time, and I want to see him stay dominant and see the Paints win." Harvey cringed as soon as he said it, realizing he sounded like a manager assessing a player's performance in a post-game press conference.

Trent narrowed his eyes into slits, and the muscles in his beefy neck tightened.

"I didn't mean any harm by it, sir. Honestly."

Trent looked over at Regina. "My boy's a good pitcher. He made the all-state team in high school as a *freshman*. Owns the school record for strikeouts by a starting pitcher. He's one of the best pitchers to ever play at Ohio University. Brian had one of the lowest ERAs of any starting pitcher in school *history*." He wagged a finger at Harvey and Amanda. "He's going to be in the major leagues someday. And soon. Remember that!"

Trent slowly turned around, and Harvey wiped some sweat from his upper lip as the muscles in his chest and back relaxed. Amanda let out a long breath and slowly looked back onto the field. Harvey watched as Trent Clark settled again into his seat, shifting his weight, his shoulders bouncing.

Amanda had been watching the dugout and the exchange of signs between George Manning and his catcher.

Brian Clark removed his cap and wiped the sweat from his brow as he toed the rubber strip running along the top of the pitcher's mound. Nathan Turner looked over at George Hanning in the dugout. George ran his hands all over his body, touching his arms, nose, and wrists with his fingers. Nathan would have to decipher the code. The sign from the manager was clear for Brian Clark.

"Changeup," Amanda blurted out. "Turner has called for a changeup."

Trent tossed a quick look over his shoulder. "This isn't his best pitch. What the heck is going on?"

This time, Harvey remained silent. He looked over to see Amanda's eyes darting back and forth between the mound and Micah Camerillo at home plate. Regina, meanwhile, took out her cell phone and swiped a finger across the glass screen shimmering under the blazing sun. When the phone blinked to life, her thumbs went to work.

Trent called back to them. "Here is some accurate information about my son, Harvey boy. The changeup is *not* his best pitch. Why is that?" he asked rhetorically.

Harvey blinked but didn't respond.

"Young pitchers like my boy, still learning to throw a variety of pitches correctly, need some seasoning before they learn to get the changeup to move across the plate in seconds. If he can't get the movement to happen on the pitch, and it's not thrown properly, any good hitter could smack it for a home run." He looked back to the field and pointed. "And that son of a gun is a good hitter." Trent huffed. "And that, Harvey boy, is a true weakness with my son and his pitching, and what he can and can't do." With that, Trent turned back around and started clapping.

A hot breeze stirred inside the ballpark, blowing some dislodged hot dog wrappers and empty peanut bags and napkins through the aisles and near the steps climbing up from the lower bowl of seats.

The pings and chimes of received and sent text messages kept trilling from Regina Carter's cell phone. Harvey looked over to Regina while Amanda was fixed on the phone. At one point, Regina held up the phone and squinted, trying to read the messages through the sunlit glare on the screen.

Annoyed at the presence of Brian Carter's parents and still stinging from the criticism from Trent Carter, Harvey wanted to sit back in his seat and pout. Instead, a fleeting thought crossed his mind, and he wanted to make sure Trent knew it.

"Hanning has called for the changeup because Micah will have to guard all corners of the plate. Brian tried coming inside on him twice with two pitches, and Hanning figures Micah expects a fastball down the middle of the plate so the count doesn't move to three balls and no strikes."

Trent huffed and then folded his arms. "Let's see what happens, Harvey boy."

Another two dings rang out from the phone as Regina Carter furiously pressed buttons with her two thumbs. Amanda removed her cell phone and stared down at it, tossing up quick glances at Regina. Trent ignored his wife.

As Brian stood on the mound, stiff and still, ready to deliver the pitch, Micah Camerillo gnawed on a wad of bubble gum and waited. Brian set and delivered, throwing a changeup toward the outside corner of the plate. Micah appeared surprised by the pitch and was slow in moving his bat from his shoulder to make contact with the baseball. The result was a pop fly. The ball towered straight up into the air beside Nathan Turner, who shielded his eyes with his glove for a few seconds before reaching up and squeezing the ball for the final out of the inning.

"Hot dog, that's it, son! That's it!" Trent hollered, jostling Regina with a forearm to her shoulder. She shot Trent a stern look and continued to ferociously tap the cell phone screen.

Harvey dropped his head and let out a long breath. George Hanning and, for that matter, Trent Clark had been right. Brian had escaped the inning.

Trent stood up, his bulky frame blocking Harvey's view of the field, and he clapped and whistled as Brian walked off the mound. Harvey stood up and sidestepped Trent, hovering in the aisle as the Paints' players trotted off the infield, all taking turns slapping and touching Brian as signs of encouragement.

When Harvey looked over at Amanda, she had paid no attention to what took place. Instead, she had removed her phone and was pressing the top of the screen with her thumbs, trying to keep pace with Regina Carter. To Harvey, they resembled two people engaged in a texting contest, and the rules only applied to them.

Trent let out a satisfied sigh as he nestled himself back into his chair. Regina continued to text, and Harvey sat down next to Amanda.

"What are you doing?"

Amanda ignored him.

"The most exciting play of the game just happened. I look over, and all I see is her texting and my wife watching."

Amanda stopped texting and put one finger over her lips.

"Oh, come on," Harvey said. "I'm getting silenced now?"

Amanda leaned to the right and caught another glimpse of Regina's cell phone and then nodded silently to herself. She leaned back into her seat, tossed a sidelong look at Harvey, who prepared to say something, but she cut him off.

"What a way to battle through it," Amanda called out. "Brian did great. I think that calls for a celebration."

Regina stopped texting for a moment and sat her cell phone down in her lap. Trent looked back at Amanda with a skeptical gaze.

"Mr. and Mrs. Carter, let Harvey and I buy us all a round. Beer okay?"

Trent deferred to Regina, who smacked her lips. "A beer does sound good."

"Make it two," Trent said, holding up two fingers.

Harvey watched the exchange, mouth agape, when Amanda pinched him on the arm. "Let's go, honey. The next half-inning starts soon."

She led him up the aisle, past a few more pockets of fans dotting the seats in the lower bowl of Veterans Administration Memorial Stadium.

Amanda stood in the shadows, her face and neck still glowing in the shade as the sunlight had bronzed her pretty features.

"Amanda, what's going on?"

"She's having an affair."

Harvey made a face. "What? Who is having an affair?"

"Regina Carter."

Harvey took a moment to let the words resonate and then scrunched his brow.

"Wait a minute. How do you know that?"

Amanda crossed her arms. "Her cell phone."

"Her cell phone?"

"Stay with me here, Harvey," Amanda said, annoyed. "Regina has not been paying attention to her son pitching or her obnoxious husband because of the cell phone."

"Here, take the beer. Let's go have a toast with the Carters, and then, we need to leave."

"Wait, what?"

Amanda gave Harvey the beer and tugged him by the wrist. "Come on. I'll explain later."

By the time they returned to the stands, the Bluesox players were scampering onto the field, taking their positions along the infield and outfield. Amanda and Harvey raced back to their seats behind home plate. When they arrived Trent was alone, swirling the remnants of the beer in his cup. Regina was gone.

They quickly toasted Brian. Amanda served as the emcee, pronouncing a dedication to Brian and his continued success as well as more wins for the Chillicothe Paints. A nervous Harvey looked on as the program protruded from under her arm.

As the Paints batter emerged from the dugout holding his bat, Amanda removed the program and opened it, then ripped out a page from it and laid it on the seat next to Trent where Regina had been sitting.

Amanda shot a wild-eyed look at Harvey. "Let's go. Now!"

Trent casually looked down at the paper as Amanda pushed her hands into Harvey. "Move it!"

Harvey awkwardly pulled himself up from the seat and nearly stumbled in the aisle with Amanda right on his heels.

She raced past him, up the aisle, and through the concourse to an exit near the back of the ballpark. Harvey called out questions to Amanda, but she ignored him.

Finally, through gasps of breath, Amanda turned around and pushed the hair back from her forehead. Harvey leaned forward, resting his hands on his thighs.

"Why did we need to run like that?"

Amanda sucked in a breath and swallowed. "Because that note I laid on the seat told Trent his wife is cheating on him and he should check her cell phone."

Princess

Edna pressed the tip of the fire iron square into Dakota's chest, and her eyes flared.

"That man," she cried, pointing with her chin to the house across the street. "That man poisoned my Princess. I know it."

Dakota looked down at the hooked metal tip pressed into his chest and eyed the small, wrinkled hands that held it. The spider veins in her wrists and fingers pulsed and twitched the tighter she gripped the handle.

Dakota took a moment to regard her measure.

"I'll need to investigate, Ms. Bruce," Dakota said, in a drawn out southern drawl. "I will speak to—"

"He's got nothing to say for himself," she barked in a crackly voice, heat flaring in the recesses of her dark green pupils. "My Princess loves everybody, and everybody loves her, except him. Except for that man."

"I understand the two of you have had some problems in the past, but I promise that I—"

"Oh, phooey," Edna said. "I don't want to talk to you, anyway. Where's the girl? She's been here before and understands my problems."

"Erin will be here soon. She's talking to Mr. Fanning as we speak."

"What's your name again?"

"Dakota Ross. I am the chief investigator with the Supp County Society of the Prevention of Cruelty to Animals."

Edna jerked her head to the side, dismissing the information, and her gaze peered over his shoulder to the house across the street. Dakota turned his head and followed her gaze. The sky was burnished pink, and the prongs of the arching limbs from the tree-lined street looked as if they might puncture a hole in the sky.

Dakota looked back at Edna, who blinked back the tears that had welled up in her eyes.

"My Princess. She's such a good dog, and she will be scared all alone. I can't imagine what she is thinking." Edna choked off her words and lowered the iron.

A palpable sense of relief washed over Dakota.

She wagged her curled finger at Dakota. "That Tim Fanning, he's such a cruel man. Always throwing things at my Princess all because she goes across the street." Edna swiped the back of her bony hand across her lip and sniffled.

"Have you ever put Princess on a leash or restrained her in any way when she goes outside?"

Edna looked at Dakota as if he spoke a foreign language. "No. She never leaves the yard except to go across the street into the woods and do her business."

Dakota nodded. Her response made the situation more complicated.

"Besides, he's threatened to hurt Princess, but I never imagined he would do it."

A large tear dribbled down her cheek. Dakota watched the waifish woman as she seemed to shrink smaller in front of him.

"And how long has Princess been missing?"

"Three days," she replied softly. "She always comes right back after she goes across the street. She is never gone long."

"Does Princess come if you call her name?"

"Yes."

Dakota nodded. "We will find Princess."

Edna turned, the loose bottom of her pink nightgown billowing as she stepped back. She leaned the fire iron against the wall gently as if the metal rod would jab a hole through it.

"I know."

Dakota had been balancing himself on the metal rise of the doorway for several minutes, and he stepped back onto the porch. He settled a look on the old woman. The lines in her face were deep and saggy, and her eyes, likely once lively, had dulled with age. Her wiry gray hair was pulled up tightly in a bun, and it matched her slouched and thin exterior.

As Dakota thought about what to say next, a gunshot rang out from behind him. He instinctively crouched down and crab walked behind one of the porch columns.

"Lordy, he's shot a gun. I'm calling the police," Edna cried out and slammed the front door shut.

Dakota leaned around the wide porch column. The house that belonged to Tim Fanning sat at the end of the road, a vast expanse of terrain that resembled more of an open prairie than a neighborhood.

Dakota felt his heart hammering painfully in his chest. As he peered around the porch column, his breathing went from fast to labored to nothing at all. Dakota felt numb. Before he could think, he took off running. His feet pounded the pavement as one thought after the other swarmed his mind.

How did all of this happen?

A warm sensation splashed onto his face as he crossed the street. The breeze made the fallen leaves rustle as they blew against the cracked pavement and chipped curbs of the street. Clouds began to flow around the sun and dapple the faint pink sky.

Dakota settled his gaze on the ranch house that belonged to Tim Fanning. It had a low-pitched, hipped roof that contained open gaps without any shingles. The faded blue siding was so badly caked in dirt and grime that the outside color looked splotchy. The front of the house had a wide-eave overhang, and large picture windows were covered with a milky film, most likely from a lack of cleaning.

He found the attached carport to the left of the house and saw a metal fence running along the width of the house into the woods. A small metal gate had been pushed back.

"Supp County SPCA!" Dakota sucked in a breath as he stood near the rear of the gate. "Erin? Mr. Fanning?"

Dakota waited for a beat, and he heard another gunshot.

"Get off my property!"

The voice was male—young and harsh but wispy in tone. The voice sounded like it came from someone who had damaged his throat in some way and emanated loudly from behind the house.

"Mr. Fanning—" Another voice. Female. "We're back here, Dakota."

He pushed ahead to find Erin standing, arms extended from her body and hands turned outward.

Erin turned her head to Dakota. "I told him we weren't armed."

Tim Fanning stood in front of Erin, lean and taut like a knife blade, holding a SIG pistol in his hand. Two white and brown spotted pit bulls lay crouched around his feet, growling with displeasure.

"It's okay," Dakota said, creeping alongside Erin with an extended open hand. "Erin and I are just here to ask you a couple of questions about Princess, Mr. Fanning. That's the dog that belongs to—"

Tim waved his arm loosely in the air. "Princess? That stupid mutt that belongs to that hag across the street?"

Tim leveled the gun at them, his face twisted with aggravation.

Dakota remained calm. "What about the dog?"

Erin cut a sharp look at Dakota. Her hazel eyes had grown hard, and strands of her ponytailed chestnut hair hung loosely over her face.

"Do you know where Princess is or what she looks like?" Dakota asked with a quaver in his voice.

"Yeah. A brown Akita. White on its paws and chest. It comes over here all of the time, attacks my dogs and craps and pisses on my property."

Dakota looked down to see the dogs, their jaws set tight, and nostrils flared, glowering at Dakota and Erin. Dakota imagined those two dogs did most of the attacking.

"I ain't seen that dog."

Dakota took another step forward. "Ms. Bruce thinks you might have hurt her dog."

Tim's lips formed into a thin line. "I love dogs, but I hate that old witch, and I hate that dog, but I never touched it. I told her to keep it on a leash, but she doesn't listen too good."

Dakota and Erin exchanged glances. "Can we take a look around, Mr. Fanning? If we can find Princess, this whole matter will be over."

Erin nodded her head dramatically. "We can look for her together and clear this up."

Tim chewed on the inside of his lip, his eyes darting back and forth between them. "Fine. Make it quick. If that stupid dog ain't here, this had better be the last time I see either of you."

Erin stepped closer to Tim. "Mr. Fanning, you told me earlier that Princess always runs to the same place when she crosses the street. Why don't you can show us the path she takes?"

Tim huffed and dropped the SIG to his side. His head whipped to the left. He squinted. "It goes down that path, near the tree line. Why, I don't know."

Erin and Dakota exchanged glances. Dakota moved first, heading for the path.

"This better be quick," Tim called out. "I want you people off my property. Pitt plays WVU at six, and I don't want to miss it!"

Tim whistled and the two pit bulls dropped their heads and slinked along behind him into the house.

Erin looked relieved as she slumped her shoulders and waited for Tim to walk past. Tim looked over at them, held a glare for a long moment, then walked past him and through the open fence gate.

Dakota slowly turned around and watched his elongated shadow slink along the house and then shrink. He wanted to make sure Tim wouldn't do anything else.

The air began to get colder now as a gust sent a chill over Dakota.

Dakota looked over the backyard. It was wide and flat with a canopy of trees lining the outer ridge of the yard. The long, arching limbs appeared to stand guard over the property. The fiery orange and blazing yellow leaves on the tree branches bathed the scene in blistering, bold color.

He looked up as rays of amber sunlight danced across his face. To the left, Dakota saw a rutted path that cut a sideways curve into the woods.

"I'm afraid this isn't going to be good," Erin said as she slowly followed Dakota down the path.

"I feel the same way."

Dakota sauntered over to the path and crouched down to the ground, trying to get down to the same level as a dog. He listened closely. The wind rustled the branches.

Erin stopped walking for a moment. Dakota could hear her breathing behind him.

"These woods are too dense and thick. A dog wouldn't go into them just to pee. Princess probably wondered down this path."

Dakota nodded. As he scanned the scene, he heard a cry. It was weak and impish, but it was a piercing break in the silence.

Dakota listened for it again. The sound returned but fainter. He whistled. "Princess."

A beat passed. No more noise.

Dakota whistled again, this time longer and with a higher pitch. "Princess. Here, girl."

As if responding, the whine returned.

As Dakota pushed ahead, the ground beneath his feet was soft and forgiving. He looked down to see fresh, indented impressions in the ground.

Someone or something has been back here recently.

Dakota pushed ahead. Erin quickened her pace. Above him, the boughs of leaves hung high in the branches above him, blocking some of the sunlight and resembling a roof that closed in around him.

At the end of the path, Dakota saw a steel fence with barbed wire crisscrossed across the top. To the right, a rusted, square metal box was attached to a long, silver pole that served as one of the support poles to the fence.

When he looked closer, his stomach clenched.

Inside the barbed wire fence were a variety of dogs of different sizes and colors. A yellow Labrador, overly thin and emaciated, charged the fence and let out a growl, its teeth bared and the hackles on its neck rising instantly. Another large brown dog charged the fence, its pitched whine being heard above the growl.

Dakota froze in front of the fence and slowly crouched down. The Labrador's gaze followed him, and the growls increased.

As Dakota glanced at the brown dog, it had a dramatic waistline, and its abdomen was sharply tucked. In the far right corner of the cage, a dog lay on its side, protecting something behind it.

A terrier mix puppy wandered up to the fence. The Labrador stopped growling for a second and nosed it. Dakota was horrified to see the terrier puppy missing one eye and droplets of blood pooling out from its mouth.

Erin gasped. "Oh, my gosh."

Dakota turned and looked back at her. "This is really bad."

Erin swallowed. "I'm going back to the truck to get some equipment. We are going to need all of the supplies we've got."

"Be careful, but hurry."

Dakota turned his attention back to the fence. Beyond it was basically an outdoor pen of starving and sick dogs. Dakota quickly counted twenty dogs running and scurrying around the ground, weaving around one another. Dakota saw no food or water bowls anywhere in the cage.

To the left of the path, Dakota saw a thin stick with a broad base. He needed something to get the dogs to back away from the fence so he could take a closer look.

He snatched the stick and held it up. The three dogs arched their heads back, eyes locked solely on the stick. Dakota pulled his arm back and launched the stick over the fence.

All the dogs began barking and sprinting to the back of the cage. The few seconds of distraction allowed Dakota a chance to enter the cage.

He approached the rusted box, looking for a button or a handle. Seeing nothing, he slammed his hand into the face of it in frustration. A snap echoed from the box, and the gate loosened.

Dakota charged into the space. The dogs, now bored with the stick, came prancing up to him. They all looked up at him, panting with lolled tongues. Dakota looked down and could count the individual rib bones on each dog.

He pushed back the pile as they curled around his feet. Dakota moved slowly to keep his balance and avoid stepping on the dogs' feet. As he moved into the middle of the cage, he saw a large brown Akita, lying on its side, panting.

Princess.

Dakota heard something behind him moving along the rutted path near the dog pen. Without taking his eyes away from Princess, he assumed Erin had come to find him.

"Erin! I've got Princess. She's right here!" he called back. "She's in bad shape. Come help me!"

The patter of footsteps stopped. Dakota slowly crouched to the ground again. A large, open wound bled onto the dog's skin, and pinkish tissue stuck out of the whole, coagulating with the blood to make a terrible scene and an awful smell. Princess didn't look at Dakota, but instead, she stared ahead with an icy glare that made Dakota pulse with anger.

Dakota removed a rag from his pocket and pressed it over the wound. Princess tensed for a moment but didn't stop panting or shift her gaze.

From behind, Dakota heard a loud click. He looked back to the front of the fence to find the slightly ajar gate now closed.

"Hey!" Dakota ran up to the fence. "Erin? Mr. Fanning?"

Other than the barking dogs behind him, Dakota couldn't see or hear anyone. He looked again for a button or switch on the rusted box then slapped it with a hand, but nothing happened. Dakota took his fist and punched it again. Still, the gate didn't move.

Dakota heard a scream. "Dakota!"

Dakota called out. "Erin. I'm back here!"

"He's coming…"

Before Dakota could say anything else, he heard a muffled scream followed by a high-pitched whistle. It was similar to the one used by Tim Fanning earlier.

Two of the larger dogs in the pen charged Dakota from behind, just below the bend of his knee. The jolt caught Dakota by surprise and knocked him off balance. He fell into the fence, one arm pressing into the honeycombed metal to brace the fall.

Dakota felt a charge surge through his body, making him feel like his insides were on fire.

Sparks flew, followed by another loud snap and then a buzz. From his side vision, Dakota could see the lean shadow of Tim Fanning with a menacing grin on his face.

Dakota tried to speak before his muscles gave way. *I'm going to be caged in here just like Princess*, he thought. Then, darkness.

Old Lady

Rachel felt Mason caress her face with his hand.

She glared into his eyes. Rachel loved many aspects of Mason and found so much of him to be beautiful, but his eyes made him the most handsome. From them came an intensity, an honesty, and a gentleness that aroused her and made her feel safe. The lines on his face deepened as he looked at Rachel like she was the most beautiful and most important person in the whole world.

Mason had torn her sundress and pulled it over her shoulders. Rachel now waited to feel how his lips would move across hers with a kiss and her body ached with anticipation for how his hands would slide across the curves of her frame. With each touch and each stroke of his thick fingers, she felt his passion for her.

As Mason searched her face, his earnestness was revealed with each twitch. He kissed her passionately, and Rachel parted her mouth slightly, allowing Mason's tongue to dance and twist with her own. She moaned with pleasure as his fingers slowly traipsed up the soft part of her thigh just above the bend in her knee. Her breath caught tightly in her throat.

Mason pushed the blue amulet necklace Rachel wore to the side, exposing the deep cleft at the base of her neck where only the thin, tan neckband draped around her throat.

As Mason moved his mouth to her neck and began nibbling on the side of her ear, Rachel welcomed the feel of his hands moving lower. As Mason moved his mouth away from her ear, and down the wide part of her neck to her breasts, she suddenly tensed.

Mason stopped kissing her and his hand froze. He slowly pulled back from her, his lips wet with spittle and the sweat from her own skin.

"What's wrong?" he asked, panting through the words.

Rachel made a face. "Nothing. Nothing at all. Don't stop." Even during foreplay, she enunciated her syllables with the crispness of a public speaker.

Mason often wondered what he did to deserve being with a woman so well spoken and beautiful. Mason looked at Rachel, not out of weakness or trite politeness but with concern. "Did I do something…did I hurt you?"

"No, no," she said, reaching an arm around his muscular back and stroking the freckled skin with her fingers. She pushed herself back away from him with an elbow until the back of her head nearly hit the headboard. "I need to get up," Rachel said with finality, indicating their afternoon tryst was over.

Mason let Rachel squirm away from under him as he swung his weight to the left, situating himself to one side and resting his head on his forearm.

"Thinking about Peter again?"

Rachel had raced over to the dresser in front of her closet. She angled herself in front of the mirror and frantically pressed her hands over the front of her legs, smoothing out the creases and red pressure marks on her skin in an attempt to massage away any remnants of their sexual dalliance.

Rachel normally felt pert and trim, but after intimate encounters with Mason—whether they had sex or not—she felt sturdy and had difficulty containing an inner giggle. She pushed her honey-gold hair back over her shoulders and pursed her thin lips. Her sour expression softened by the experience of being with Mason.

"No, I wasn't thinking about Peter," she replied sharply. "I don't think about him every time we are together."

"Just most of the time." Mason sighed and pushed himself off the bed. He slowly collected his jeans and slipped one leg into the open pant leg.

Mason stood up tall then slicked back his hair. After buttoning his jeans, he tucked both hands into the side pockets. His sun-dyed hair and tanned skin drew out the creases of his chiseled physique.

"Please, don't be upset with me. I'm just not ready."

Mason cut a sidelong glance at her. "It's fine."

"No, I can tell by your tone that it's not fine."

Mason blinked. "I'm trying to understand, Rachel. I really am. But it's been three years since Peter died, and we've been together for over a year. I just wish—" His voice trailed away, causing Rachel's face to flush.

"Wish what, Mason? That I could just *move on*?"

Mason seemed wounded at the remark. He pulled the mesh sweater over his head and pushed his arms through the sleeves. "No. Don't start with that. I can never begin to imagine the pain and heartbreak of losing a spouse. Don't put words in my mouth."

Before Rachel could speak again, he cut her off. "I want to be able to give myself to you completely, and I want you to be able to do that for me. That's all. I'm not trying to take Peter's place or be the same type of lover he was, but—" He looked away. "That stupid necklace. Every time I see it, I realize that maybe *you* aren't ready to move on and give me a chance."

Rachel bristled. "This necklace is one of the last things Peter gave me before he died. Wearing it helps me feel close to him."

Rachel realized the mistake as soon as she said it.

"Mason, I'm sorry. I didn't mean—"

He stalked across the room and brushed past her. "That's exactly what I'm talking about."

He'd removed his sandals and left them by the front door, which was always a requirement when visiting Rachel. He grabbed the arched handle on the oak-paneled front door and pulled back. The air was fresh and bracing in the lungs.

As Mason stepped off the porch and onto the slate-covered front step, he felt Rachel's hand on his shoulder.

She tried to stop his charge and pull him back inside, but Mason was firm and rigid.

"I don't want to end the night fighting," she said, the words sounding more of a plea instead of a declarative statement. "Come back inside, and we can talk about it."

Mason felt a pang of guilt burn in his stomach. He hated ending anything in an argument, especially time spent with Rachel. They had been fighting more lately and many of their conversations and evenings together ended with them slinging acrimonious words and accusations at one another. This time, Mason held his ground.

"I need to go," he said softly, not looking back.

The sun was falling behind the horizon of the mountains that bracketed her home, painting the sky in shades of red and pomegranate pink. Rachel slipped through a narrow slit of the contrasting bands of light made by the sunset and the white light emanating from the foyer and squeezed past Mason just below his ribcage. His elbow nearly slapped the top of her head.

She swept around in front of him like a flash, tossing tufts of her hair behind her. "Don't do this!"

"Do what, Rachel?"

"Leave like this. Please. I want you. I want to be with you, to give myself completely to you." She stopped speaking as if a hitch in her throat had cut off the words.

Mason peered down at her with a sympathetic look bereft of anger. He cupped a hand lightly around her shoulder. The reflection and refraction of the sun on the amulet heightened the rich blue hue of the diamond. It brought the sadness and frustration Mason had brushed aside for the moment back to the surface of his thinking.

"What I am talking about is what just happened."

Rachel furrowed her thin eyebrows in confusion.

Mason took in a deep breath. "When we have a fight, your love and devotion are always reaffirmed to me and just when I start to really believe and feel the words, something happens. It's like there is always a large 'but' at the end of it."

"Mason—"

"It's getting late, Rachel. I've had a long day at work, and I really want to spend time together, but maybe I'm just tired and not thinking clearly."

Rachel flashed him an offended look, one mixed with hurt.

Mason's pastel-blue eyes flickered as he leaned down and kissed her lightly on the lips. "I'll call tomorrow."

Shoulders slumped dejectedly, Mason walked down the steps, his broad shoulders and muscular back framed in the pink light before being swallowed up by the shadows beyond her sight.

She heard the door of his truck slam shut, then the engine clicked and rolled over as Mason threw the car into reverse and sped backward down the driveway.

Rachel closed the door behind her. The adrenaline rush of foreplay, an anticipated climax, and then the terse exchange with him over the exact state of their relationship left her exhausted and her body limp, as if all of her muscles had atrophied. She made her way back upstairs and looked at the rumpled sheets. The smell of Mason, a mix of sweat and earthy cologne, hung in the air.

Rachel flopped down on the bed and pressed the heels of her hands over her eyes. She groaned aloud as the amulet flopped over her collarbone.

As Rachel was collecting her thoughts, her cell phone dinged on the nightstand. She considered letting it cycle through to voicemail but draped her arm over the edge of the bed and wiggled across the mattress until she snared the phone.

Before Rachel could say a word, a loud baritone voice exploded through the line. "Mom?"

"Hi, Keith."

"Mom, I've been calling for two hours. Is everything okay?"

Rachel cringed for a moment. She and Mason hated to be distracted by anything when they were together, so she had silenced her phone.

"I'm sorry, honey." Rachel sat up on the edge of the bed. The mattress sat so high up on the bed frame that her feet didn't touch the floor. "Things have been busy at work." Her feet swayed in the air as she spoke. "I meant to call."

"We always talk on Thursdays," Keith said, sounding like a disappointed toddler that didn't get the toy he wanted instead of the well-adjusted twenty-three-year-old she and Peter had raised.

"I know, honey. It's my fault. Mason was here, and—"

She realized the mistake the minute she said it. Mason was on her mind, and she couldn't help but mention his name.

Static crossed the line for a moment. "Mason was there?"

"Yes."

Rachel could picture the excitement on her son's face. "That's good. That's really good, Mom. I am so glad I got to meet him at the Fourth of July picnic. I wish I could come home more often and get to know him better.

"Don't be silly, honey. Concentrate on your classes at Penn State."

"But, Mom, he's a really good dude, and he's *really* into you."

She felt her cheeks blush pink. "I know, and I like him, too." The hesitation in her voice returned, and Keith jumped on it.

"But what, Mom? Please, don't tell me Dad is interfering."

The flippant way Keith made the remark, as if Peter were in the next room plotting something to keep her and Mason apart, made Rachel chuckle.

"No, it's not that. It's just...I love Mason. I really do. He loves me, and I know it." The words came out in spurts as if Rachel was prepared to justify her feelings.

"Did you have a fight?"

Keith was perceptive and intuitive like Peter had been.

"It wasn't a fight." Rachel became defensive. "It's just...this is ridiculous. I'm not going to talk to my son about this."

"Mom—"

"I'm fine. Mason and I are fine. Tell me what's going on at school. How are classes? It's nearly midterm, right?"

"Don't change the subject." It was Keith's turn to be defensive.

"I'm not. I really want to know how my son is doing."

Keith responded as if he hadn't been listening. "Promise me something, Mom. Please, don't let Dad ruin things with Mason. Dad would not want you spending the rest of your life alone and not getting laid."

"Keith! Please." Her son was also blunt like Peter. "I can do without the explicit language."

"What I'm saying, Mom, is don't give up something that is really great, and Mason seems really great."

Another wave of exhaustion swept over her. "Fine, I will."

"Promise?"

"I promise."

Rachel didn't remember much else of the conversation as Keith prattled on about why the Penn State–Wisconsin football game on Saturday was critical to the success of the Nittany Lions' football season and why his calculus professor sounded like one of the characters on *The Simpsons* when he lectured. The words Keith said earlier coupled with what Mason had said about her proclivity to think about Peter when they were together roiled in her mind like a rugged ocean tide, and the churning of the words and emotions had left her nauseous in the pit of her stomach.

When Keith finally stopped, Rachel told him she loved him and promised to talk with him next Thursday.

A cold chill overcame Rachel and made her teeth chatter. She looked down. Basically naked without a bra and her panties, Rachel rubbed her bare shoulders with her arms and strode over to the closet again, refusing to examine herself in the mirror. She reached into the top drawer, snatched a new bra, and put it on. She found a pink chiffon round-necked, long-sleeved blouse and slipped it on then put on some dark jeans that had been wadded up and tossed into the corner of the closet. Rachel didn't plan on going anywhere else that evening, but she wasn't ready to put on her nightclothes yet.

When she arrived back downstairs, she reached into the refrigerator and pulled out some milk then eyed the coffee pot sitting on the counter. Rachel prided herself on only needing one cup of coffee to make it through the day, but given the circumstances surrounding the evening, the warmth and creaminess of coffee sounded soothing to her.

She reached into the cabinet above and pulled down the blue coffee tin. The ease with which she was able to lift it from the shelf made her curse under her breath. Rachel was out of coffee.

She slammed the empty can on the counter and chewed on a fingernail for a moment. No other beverage, not even alcohol, sounded satisfying to her at that moment. She tossed her head back and stared at the low-hanging light rack. Rachel groaned and grabbed her purse from a chair near the kitchen island.

When Rachel reached the front door, she swallowed hard. She could still feel Mason's presence and sensed the anguish in his voice as he told her he was leaving. The thought made her mind foggy. For a moment, Rachel forgot why she was standing there clutching her car keys in a clenched fist.

Outside, the sky had changed to a pale shade of orange, and the clouds had turned translucent and pink, almost as if blushing under the rays of the descending sun. A chilly breeze wafted past her, smelling of earth and decaying leaves.

As Rachel hopped into her gray Mercedes, she thought about coupons and if she had clipped any from the Sunday *Lexington Herald-Leader* newspaper. She preferred shopping at Meijer for coffee anyway, and the prices were lower.

The house sat at the base of a gravel path in Collins Court that trailed away from the main intersection of West Main Avenue. The entire driveway was bracketed by a cherry row of townhouses that had lush vines and shrubs surrounding the entrance to each porch.

Rachel turned onto West Main Avenue. She loved parts of her life. Her job as an IT administrator with Integrity IT in Lexington provided her with a good salary and benefits and allowed her to send Keith to Penn State—a school he'd loved since he was a kid—without forcing him to take out student loans. Living in Richmond, Kentucky provided a slower-paced life than the more metropolitan Lexington, and it provided her the solace and comfort she needed after watching a debilitating stroke reduce her once athletic, active husband into a man who couldn't feed himself and didn't recognize the names or faces of his own family.

She whipped the Mercedes into the mostly empty parking lot at Meijer. Known for its fresh food and for being a family-owned business, Rachel preferred it to a chain grocery store like Kroger or Walmart.

Rachel sprang out of the car and passed an exhausted-looking mother with dark crescents under her eyes loping near the back of her small car while a baby screamed a high-pitched wail inside the car. She remembered those shopping trips with Keith and was glad *that* part of her life was over.

The Richmond Meijer store was a typical supermarket. The food sections were to the left of the entrance, and the general merchandise section was off to the right. From ten feet away, the smell of freshly baked bread wafted over to the main aisle. Cashiers stood lazily by the registers while employees paced around the stores, carrying cleaning supplies and discarded items left in wrong places by customers. A flashing, lighted sign with a large, white number seven encircled in red caught Rachel's attention. She burst down the aisle and spun on her heel and froze.

Mason stood midway down the aisle on the right side, looking at bottles of coffee creamer, which were next to the section of the blue Maxwell House blend that Rachel was craving like an addict who needed another fix.

Rachel caught her breath. There was no way she would be able to go down the aisle without Mason seeing her. She stood up straight, collected herself, and marched confidently down the aisle.

Mason was studying the ingredients label of one of the containers when he sensed someone approaching. He cut a sideways look at Rachel then looked away. He blinked and then looked up again to see Rachel moving down the aisle, a burst of wind tickling his neck.

He coughed once. When Rachel ignored him, he did it again, only this time louder and more obvious.

Rachel stopped and dropped her head. She slowly turned around and held up her hand and made a faint wave.

"Out of coffee," she said in an impish voice that sounded like a schoolgirl that had run into her crush.

Mason looked her over and nodded then slowly gazed back at the coffee creamer label.

Rachel felt the silence build between them. A cacophony of bleeping cash registers and rickety metal buggies moving aggressively down neighboring aisles was all that filled the space.

"I don't want it to be like this," Rachel said, feeling compelled to step closer to Mason.

He carefully placed the creamer back on the shelf and puffed out his chest. He slowly turned to her, his face placid and expressionless. He was wearing a black sweater now and brown corduroy pants with brown shoes. He looked amazing.

"I don't either, Rachel. Which is why it's over."

Those words left Rachel feeling gut-punched. "What's over?"

He looked at her with the pathetic stare of someone who felt sorry for her. "Us, Rachel. We are over."

"Mason, I don't understand."

He held up a hand, and Rachel could see the ridges in between his stubby fingers. "Let me finish. I've been driving around all evening since I left your place thinking about our fight and what didn't happen tonight between us. I just think it's not fair to either of us."

Rachel felt anger welling up inside her. "Stop speaking in code, Mason." She stomped her foot. "Say what you mean."

"I mean, I need to give you space to completely move on from Peter, and you need to give me a chance to be with someone who wants to be with me. All of me. Emotionally, physically, everything. It hurts me that there is a part of you that shuts me out when we are together."

Rachel felt sideswiped again. "I can change, Mason. Like you said, it's been three years. Maybe now I am ready to move on. And I want to move on with you."

The words poured out of her with an urgency that made her lips quiver.

Mason closed his eyes and shook his head. "Rachel, I've heard a variation of that so many times, and then the next time we are together, nothing changes."

His gaze lowered onto the diamond amulet, and as he stared at it for a second, Rachel felt guilty for not taking it off when she put on her clothes.

"I love you, Rachel. I really do. And I love you enough to know that for you to heal, I need to be out of your life. I just can't be with someone who doesn't trust me enough to let me all the way in."

Rachel felt desperate and sad, and a burning sensation came up through her lungs as her heart began to throb in her chest. She reached her hands out to him for an awkward embrace.

Mason stepped backwards, hands in the air as if Rachel had drawn a weapon on him.

"Goodbye, Rachel."

With that, Mason turned and left the aisle, alone and without the coffee creamer he'd been examining. Rachel stood in stunned silence for a moment, unsure of what had transpired. In the seconds that followed, the reality hit her hard. Mason was gone and out of her life. Forever.

Rachel collapsed her back against the shelf and slid down to the floor. Her eyes were watery, and her tongue felt thick and knotty in her throat. She replayed the words in her head. *For you to heal, I need to be out of your life.* Mason had destroyed her with words, but she had done it by failing to give herself to him.

Rachel tilted her head back against the lip of the shelf, pushing some coffee cans deeper into the space. Mason was right. She was scared of intimacy with him. All he wanted was her commitment and her love, a physical connection to sustain him.

Rachel continued to sob quietly. She had become so afraid of intimacy and the vulnerability it brought that she looked for any reason to thwart the sexual heat she felt for him. *I just can't be with someone who doesn't trust me enough to let me all the way in.*

Rachel felt her tears flowing faster and her sobs getting louder and coming with more fervor. She closed her eyes and winced, wishing the day would start over so she could do everything differently.

"Hey, old lady!"

She thought the noise might be coming from somewhere else, but when she heard the unsteady loping of shoes clacking against the tile floor, Rachel forced herself to look to the left.

The child moved as if her knees were made of hinges. Dressed in a primrose, tiered crochet-necked dress, and Tiny Toms strappy sandals, she giggled, waving her arms in the air as if waiting for someone to pick her up.

From behind the little girl, a woman appeared, huffing and disheveled. She was small with brown eyes, alabaster skin, and a tiny pockmark on her forehead. The woman wore baggy jeans and a man's white T-shirt that swayed as she walked.

"Caroline, I said stop!"

The little girl kept plopping ahead. "Old lady. Old lady!" A small, curled finger covered in spit and drool seemed to wink at Rachel as the girl approached.

"No, that's not nice." The mother huffed, knitting her brow together as she reached down and hoisted her little girl against her. The girl screamed with delight and cooed as her mother stroked her brown hair with long fingers.

Rachel could see the mother's small breasts rising and falling as she tried to catch her breath. Rachel assumed a game of chase between the woman and the girl had been going on for some time.

The woman stopped near Rachel, almost as if noticing her for the first time. "I'm sorry. Please, forget what my little girl said." The woman slowly eyed Rachel, looking her over. "Are you okay, ma'am?"

Rachel wiped away some tears with the back of her hand. "I'm fine," she said, her voice barely above a croak.

The woman looked down and grinned. "If Meijer doesn't have a certain item, they can order it. There's really no need to get upset. I'm Mattie Cox, by the way." Her grin widened as if she was proud of the quip.

Rachel just looked away. "Rachel Franklin. I wish a missing item was all it was."

Rachel braced herself against the shelf and pulled herself up. As she turned around to collect herself, she saw Caroline holding her arms out, away from her mother.

"Old lady needs a hug."

Mattie grimaced as the weight of Caroline's lean loosened her grip. Rachel instinctively held out her arms, and Caroline seemed to melt into her chest.

"Why are you sad?" Caroline said in the impish voice of a little girl.

Rachel leaned back away from the girl as she cradled her against her side. "I'm fine, honey."

Caroline looked past Rachel onto the floor where Rachel had been sitting. "You fell and were crying. Mommy says not to cry too much, but try to get up."

The kernel of wisdom in the words caused Rachel to smile. It felt like the first real smile she'd flashed in a long time. "I think your mommy is very smart."

Rachel watched Mattie's face blush as she shrugged her shoulders. Caroline locked her arms around Rachel's neck and collapsed against her.

"Thank you, sweetheart," Rachel whispered, stroking the back of Caroline's hair. The little girl smelled sweet and milky.

Rachel gave Caroline one more tight squeeze. She leaned into the little girl's ear and said. "I think we'd better get you back to your mommy now."

"Okay," Caroline murmured with her lips still buried near the base of Rachel's neck.

Rachel slowly let Caroline slide down her, and then Caroline hobbled back over to Mattie, who scooped her up.

"Rachel, I'm terribly sorry. Caroline has never done that before. I am sorry she called you an old lady."

"Don't worry about it," Rachel said, waving off the comment. "It's been so long since I've had one that little. The hug brought back many good memories, and after today, I really needed it."

Mattie was ready to leave. "Well, it was nice meeting you. Come on, Caroline. Time to go home."

Rachel watched as they retreated down the aisle. "Thank you," Rachel called out to a shadow that bent and curved around the shelf before disappearing.

When Rachel made it home, she nearly collapsed in the living room chair. She managed to get the coffee she'd been craving but was now so emotionally exhausted that she could barely keep her eyes open. In the silence of the house, she could hear Mason speaking to her, wanting to know how her day went and telling Rachel how much she meant to him. Rachel could hear Peter talking, fretting over how expensive the electric bill had been during the summer and wondering why Keith never called home much while at Penn State. Rachel opened her eyes and imagined Keith, the same age as Caroline, wobbling around the living room before falling down onto his padded bottom.

Rachel closed her eyes and fought to clear her mind of the voices and concentrate on nothing for a while.

***

Something slapped up against her front door. The dull thud snapped Rachel to attention. Her arms were sore and her feet asleep, feeling like a million needles had been inserted while she slept. A thin stream of saliva had dried under her chin.

Sleep-smeared and startled, she bolted up from the chair. Her mouth was dry, and her tongue felt thick in her mouth. The living room was dark except for slatted streaks of moonlight that beamed into the bay window behind her.

Rachel cautiously moved to the front door. She turned on the overhead light in the entryway and slowly unlocked the door. When she looked down, she nearly tripped over the *Lexington Herald-Leader* newspaper that had been tossed like a wet sop against the face of the door. Rachel was usually asleep upstairs when the paper was delivered, and she wondered if tossing it against the door was the way the newspaper always made it to her house.

Rachel collected the paper and sauntered into the kitchen. Now awake, she decided to make some coffee.

After she put the water in and scooped the coffee grounds into the coffeemaker and pressed start, she sat down on a barstool at the island bench. Rachel felt her necklace bounce against the saggy fold of skin under her chin. The strap tickled her chin, which was unusual.

She reached down and tugged on the strap. That was when she noticed it. The amulet was missing.

Frantic, she touched every inch of the strap, both in front and behind her neck. Rachel's heart began to race. She swung her legs forward and hopped off the stool then turned on the lights in the kitchen and retraced her steps.

Rachel stormed through the living room, removing all the seat cushions from the furniture and looking in the narrow slits of darkness between the bottom of the furniture and the floor. Her breathing quickened, and her eyes moistened. All she could think about was how Peter gave her that amulet on their anniversary right before his stroke and how upset he would be if she'd lost it.

The coffee machine gurgled and hissed in the kitchen, but Rachel ignored it. She flew up the stairs and began taking each room apart, looking to see if maybe somehow, someway, it had fallen off.

After an hour of searching, Rachel made her way back to the living room and sat down. A flitting thought crossed her mind. *Meijer*. Rachel had been traipsing up and down the aisles of the store looking for coffee and, of course, there was the encounter with Mattie and Caroline.

Rachel checked the clock on the microwave in the kitchen. Seven in the morning. Meijer's would be open, and she could call to see if they found the amulet.

After twenty minutes of being put on hold and passed back and forth between employees and managers, the night janitor supervisor, who was getting ready to leave, came on the phone and said that he had personally cleaned the aisle where the coffee was stored, and no jewelry had been found. When Rachel angrily asked the man if anyone had checked the shelves themselves, he said no, but the shelf-stocking crew would be in at nine, and he would leave a note for them.

Rachel tossed her cell phone across the room onto the couch in frustration, trying not to be mad at anyone else other than herself. In less than one day, she had lost Mason, a wonderful man whom she loved, as well as the last piece of something given to her by the other man she loved, her husband and soul mate, Peter.

The tension grew in her face and limbs. Her eyes scanned the room in its disheveled state, and the panic inside her grew. Fresh tears stained her cheeks, and Rachel stroked the neck strap, rubbing the bottom where the amulet should be. On the couch, her cell phone chirped. Rachel walked over to pick it up, and a message flashed on her screen.

Mason: Can we talk? And soon?

The text had been sent around six. Mason was a morning person and always told Rachel he was more productive before the sun came up. Rachel was glad Mason had made her a priority during his morning routine but wondered where that concern was yesterday evening.

Another loud bang came at the front door, this one heavy and dense. Rachel had a sudden urge to run upstairs and curl herself tightly under the covers of her bed. She wondered if Mason had decided to come over to talk in person since she had ignored the text message.

Rachel brushed her hair back and licked her lips. She knew she felt and looked terrible but wanted to seem ready in some way to see Mason.

When she pulled open the door, Caroline flew through the space.

"Old Lady!"

Caroline wrapped her arms around Rachel's legs. Rachel was dumbstruck, her mouth agape. Caroline had a pink T-shirt on with blue shorts and sandals. The T-shirt rode up her back some.

"Caroline, what are you doing here, sweetheart?" When Rachel looked up, Mattie filled the space. Mattie wore the blue scrubs fitting for a hospital. Her hair was shiny, and her face smooth and accented with makeup, and she smelled sweet of lavender and vanilla.

"I'm sorry, Rachel," Mattie said, looking away. "I found your home address by doing a search of your name online. I didn't mean to come by this early. I normally take Caroline to day care during this time. Our day care center is down by the campus at EKU, and we drive right by the neighborhood. I told Caroline we'd come by later, but she insisted on coming by now."

Rachel glared at Mattie for a moment before looking down at Caroline. The little girl had stepped back and held up her hands. Rachel locked her eyes on her wide, open face.

"Hug."

Still a bit confused, Rachel bent down. "Yes, of course, honey." Rachel reached down and grabbed Caroline then lifted her up, clutching her tightly before transferring the little girl to her left hip.

"Where are my manners? Please, come in," Rachel commanded in a tone more formal than she would have liked.

They entered the foyer. Mattie's eyes grew wide as she surveyed the tossed couch cushions and clumps of dust that Rachel had shoved into the middle of the room.

Rachel cleared her throat. "I normally don't have company this early in the morning."

"I'm sure," Mattie said. "Caroline was insistent that we come now."

Rachel furrowed her brow. "May I ask why?"

Caroline squirmed against Rachel and leaned back, giggling and cooing. "Smile."

Caroline had been chewing on two fingers. She took her thin little fingers, still wet with saliva, and pressed Rachel's lips back, trying to curve them into a smile. Instead, she pressed them flat against her face.

"Caroline!" Mattie called out. "No! You don't do that."

Rachel forced a calm smile across her face. "It's fine." Rachel regarded Caroline for a moment. "Your little girl is very perceptive. I do need to smile more."

Caroline giggled and did it again. This time, Rachel was ready for the pressure and moved her lips in tandem with the pressure the little girl applied to her face.

Caroline loved it and giggled again and clapped. Rachel could feel a dull ache creeping up in her back.

Mattie studied their play closely and leaned in. "That's not the real reason we are here."

"Oh." The statement caught Rachel off guard. "Caroline, I'm going to put you down. Why don't you go into the living room so mommy and I can talk?"

Caroline gave a big, slow nod. Her eyes flickered, and she looked over at Mattie for permission.

"It's okay, Caroline. Do as Rachel says."

Caroline took a hesitant step and then bounded into the living room, jumping onto a pile of couch cushions.

Rachel watched her movements, marveling at her comfort with strangers and her energy. She wished she had some of Caroline's energy now.

When Rachel turned around, Mattie held up a white cloth, wadded in her hand.

"I think this might belong to you."

Mattie slowly removed the cloth, and the blue diamond amulet shined under the overhead light. It's reemergence and beauty brightened Rachel.

"I, uh, where did you—"

"It was Caroline," Mattie said, disappointed. "My daughter thought it was a toy around your neck. During the hug last night, she swiped it. I went back to the grocery store last night. I spoke to one of the bag boys. He said he's bagged a number of groceries for you and that you always wear that necklace." Mattie paused, expecting a fiery, accusatory response. "I promise. She didn't mean to do it. She—I mean we weren't trying to take advantage of the situation."

Rachel held up the amulet and marveled at it like she had never seen it before. She ignored the plea from Mattie. "I don't remember Caroline doing that at all."

Mattie let out a tight laugh. "I'm not surprised. You were having some problems last night."

Rachel gripped the amulet in her hand. "I know. I apologize. I don't like when my personal problems become public."

Mattie looked down, shifting her weight between her feet. "It's fine. It happens."

Rachel held a gaze with Mattie and bounced the amulet between them. "I've been frantic all morning looking for this."

She paused and turned, giving a big swiping motion into the living room. "As you can tell."

Both women laughed.

"This amulet was a gift from my husband, Peter. It's so special to me."

"I'm sure he'll be thrilled as well."

Silence hung in the air between them as Caroline started to make a fort out of the pillows in the living room.

Mattie broke the silence. "Is it something I said?"

"It's just that Peter died three years ago. This is the last gift he shared with me before I lost him."

Rachel watched as Mattie's faced blanched. "I'm so sorry. I didn't know—"

"It's fine, really." Rachel threaded the amulet back through the necklace. "I'm afraid this isn't all I've messed up recently. There is this great guy and, because I've let this amulet and my late husband come between us, I think I've lost probably the second best thing in my life next to my son."

Mattie looked at Rachel, a look of bemused confusion crossing her face.

Rachel winced. "Never mind. I'm sorry. I don't mean to use this as a therapy session. Forgive me. Thanks for returning the amulet. It means more to me than I can put into words."

Mattie and Rachel both lowered their gazes to the floor. Mattie looked up first and put her hand on Rachel's shoulder.

"I know we don't know one another well, but can I give you some advice?"

Rachel felt a connection between them at that moment. She nodded.

"My boyfriend, Jackson, was supposed to marry me. I thought we had a perfect life. We talked about having children and family and growing old together."

Rachel watched her closely.

Mattie blanched. "Then I got pregnant, and suddenly, Jackson didn't want any of that anymore. I went into a deep depression. I stopped talking to my friends, my parents. I lost my job at the University of Kentucky Medical Center and had to take a lesser-paying job at a family practice center here in

Richmond. I lost all of my happiness." Mattie took in a deep breath then exhaled as she spoke. "I wish I had reached out to people and didn't push people away. What I needed was people around me. People who loved me no matter if I was single, married, pregnant, or whatever." Mattie paused again and then pursed her lips. "I hope you can do that and be with people who love you and want to be with you. Don't be afraid to lose yourself with them. Trust me, if they want to leave, they will."

The comments felt like a rush of fresh air for Rachel.

When Mattie smiled and patted Rachel on each arm, Rachel looked away and thought for a moment then nodded her head. She thought about Mason wanting Rachel to give herself to him completely, not just sexually but also emotionally. She thought about Keith and how he had found happiness and contentment at college far away from home.

Caroline ran back to Rachel and embraced her legs. "Hug. Please."

Rachel looked down and felt her cheeks burn with love.

"Mattie, would you have time for a cup of coffee before you leave?"

Mattie didn't hesitate. "I'd love some coffee."

Rachel bent down and picked Caroline up. Her forehead was dappled with sweat from playing in the living room.

"How about this," she said, flicking the tip of Caroline's flat nose with her fingertip. "I'd like you and your mommy to come and visit this old lady more often."

Caroline clapped again. "Old Lady! I love you."

Rachel felt her heart melt and her skin flutter. "I love you, too, sweetie. I've got some cookies in the cabinet. Would you like some?"

Caroline beamed a bright grin. "Yes, please. Cookies."

Rachel motioned them into the kitchen, and as they moved, Rachel trailed behind, detouring into the living room where she picked up the cell phone.

Scrolling through her contacts list, she found Mason's number and clicked the call button.

Acknowledgments

I have always been an avid reader of short stories. As a writer, the short story genre taught me how to write and it was so much fun to revisit the genre after several years of writing novels.

Thanks to Bob Johnson, Julie Hensley, Nancy Jensen and Amanda Eyre Ward for teaching me how to read and write short stories. These stories would never have been completed without their knowledge and guidance.

My editors Kat Mazurak and Rogena Mitchell-Jones went through each line of each story and helped me revise and reshape the book into something readable and intelligible. I appreciate their efforts, including all of those late-night phone calls.

I owe a great deal to Earl Dean, Matthew Ferrence, and Laura Morris who served as early readers on the manuscript and provided wonderful feedback.

My friend and publicist Joe Walters spent so much time and effort spreading news and information about the book to so many people in so many places. Thanks for the help, Joe!

To Pam Stack and my Authors on the Air Radio Family, I owe a great deal of gratitude. All of the great folks associated with the network encouraged me to keep writing and keep working on these stories, even when life and other obstacles challenged me for time and energy.

Tiffany Gibson and the entire team at Morgan James Publishing believed in this book from the beginning and they have been its biggest advocates. They really know how to produce and market a book and their expertise has been wonderful and invaluable.

Special thanks goes to Chip and my family for allowing me to disappear for days and weeks at time to work on this book. I missed a lot of parties, dates, and other fun events to get this book done and none of them ever made me feel guilty over it.

To Carter, Laura, Cat, Lynne, Sheila, Fran, and Mickey... thanks for the support!

Lastly, I want to thank you, the reader. Time and money are precious commodities in our society today. The fact that you spent both on this book is really appreciated and not taken for granted.

Harvey was struggling to follow the story. "And this proves she's having an affair? How?"

"It's not just the cell phone. It's what she's been doing and texting on the cell phone."

Harvey stepped back, then tossed his head back for a moment and closed his eyes. "Now I get it."

Amanda tossed up her arms and let them fall helplessly at her side. "Look who's late to the party."

"But texting another man doesn't mean she's having an affair."

"The proper term is sexting."

Harvey blinked twice. "Whatever. Men and women text each other all the time."

"It wasn't just words," Amanda intoned. She led Harvey by the arm to a wall near a concession stand. "Regina was sending texts. Wanting things. Wanting to do things with this person."

"Sexual *things?*"

Amanda slapped Harvey's arm. "Yes. Sexual things. I didn't get to see everything in the text messages, but I did see that they were discussing times they could meet, and she sexted this guy and said she wanted him to pleasure her in certain ways."

"Maybe it was just a joke."

"No way," Amanda quipped. "It wasn't just the words. There were pictures, Harvey. Naked pictures of her. And he sent her naked pictures of himself."

Harvey felt his face flush. "Wow. It takes guts for Regina to send and receive pictures like that in public with her husband sitting right next to her."

"But there's more. When Regina was scrolling through the images saved on her phone, there were a couple of pictures of her and another man, locked in a romantic embrace. At first, the man in the photo didn't look familiar, but when she scrolled past him again, it hit me. The man in the picture is Matt Cora."

The name passed through Harvey's memory, and then recognition hit. "Wait. Matt Cora, the Paints' pitching coach?"

"Yep."

Harvey let out a breath. "That doesn't necessarily mean that Matt and Regina are having an affair. The players, their families, and the coaches are a tight group. This is minor league baseball, after all."

"The naked man had caramel-colored skin just like Matt. It has to be more than a coincidence."

Harvey thought about Matt Cora and how his brand of tough love had made the Paints' pitchers tougher and better over the years. Matt's tough demeanor didn't extend to his interactions with fans as he would often spend time before and after games interacting with fans and little kids who wanted to talk about baseball. He autographed any item people put in front of him.

He cocked his head to the side. "Are you sure about this?"

Amanda bit down on her lip. "I'm almost positive."

Harvey nodded.

"And we need to tell Trent."

Harvey felt his face flush. "No way. Not a chance. What Regina Carter does and who she does it with is none of our business."

"Harvey—"

He held up a hand. "No, Amanda. We barely know them, and for those few minutes earlier, I was pretty sure Trent Carter was going to turn around and hit me for criticizing his son."

Amanda placed her hands on her hips and glared at her husband. "But this involves more than just us and more than just the Carters. If she's having an affair with a coach on the team, this is really bad. I'm sure there are players on the team who know about it. As you said, these guys spend plenty of time with each other. Someone would have to know about it. It's possible Brian even knows."

Harvey felt a rush of air pass between them and a round shadow emerged from the sunlit concourse.

"What does my son know?"

Harvey felt every muscle in his body constrict with tension, and Amanda blushed.

"Mr. Carter. Sorry. Harvey and I were just talking."

Trent eyed them skeptically, the folds of skin under his eyes tightening under the look. "I thought we were going to have beers to celebrate. The next half-inning is getting ready to start."

"Oh, yes, right. I forgot." The command felt like a stinging bolt of electricity that made Harvey want to jump from his standing position. "The beers. I'm sorry. Let me go get them."

Amanda grabbed his arm and flashed an angry glance at Harvey. "I'll get them." She looked over at Trent. "I have the money anyway."

As Amanda trotted off, Trent arched a hairy eyebrow at Harvey. "Both of you are acting strangely."

Harvey cleared his throat and flashed an impish grin. "Lovers spat."

Trent twisted his lips to the side and reared back. "Who cares. What does Brian know?"

Harvey neck muscles seized. His tongue felt thick and rough in his mouth like sandpaper.

"Amanda and I were just talking about that last pitch. The changeup. I can remember Brian really struggling with that pitch early in the season, but now he's done so much better. I bet working with Matt Cora has helped." Harvey couldn't believe he had allowed Matt's name to escape from his lips. He stammered for a moment but quickly recovered. "He fired that ball in there. Heck, Micah Camerillo is probably still standing behind home plate looking for that pitch."

Trent waited a moment and then let out a laugh. "Yeah. Yeah, that's right. That little baby probably couldn't hit it now, either." Trent smacked Harvey so hard on the shoulder in between laughs it nearly knocked him against the wall.

Harvey managed to let out a little laugh then looked around, trying to find Amanda.

As Harvey looked back at Trent, Amanda returned. "Got the beers," she chirped.

Trent grabbed the plastic cup from her hand and held it up to his lips, slurping down the frothy foam.

"Ah," he said, licking his lips. "Cold beer on a hot day at the ballpark. Nothing better."

Trent turned around and disappeared. When Harvey looked at Amanda, he noticed something tucked under her arm. He made another face.

"Why do you have a game program shoved under your arm?" he asked, pointing. "We already have one."

Rhonda looked up pleadingly at Ken. He gave her a curt nod, an assurance that she needed to comply.

Rhonda took her time standing up. Dampness in the air made her shiver. A waifish court reporter with dyed-red curls and horn-rimmed glasses sat perched on the edge of her seat, fingers hovering over the keys of the stenotype, ready to transcribe the next set of spoken words. The bailiff, a Kanawha County Sheriff's Deputy, stiffened and folded his meaty hands across his waist, holding his breath and staring blankly ahead.

"Ms. Pendleton," the judge said, speaking confidently and quickly. "This is the second time you have appeared before this court. I distinctly remember telling you that any violation of your probation would land you back here, which would not be a good thing."

Rhonda nodded quickly. "Yes. Yes, Your Honor." The words came out weak, and her tongue felt dry and thick in her mouth.

"This recent violation leaves me with few options."

Rhonda lowered her gaze and nodded.

"Well?" the judge asked. "What is your reasoning for violating your probation?"

She cut a sharp look at Ken, who pressed his lips together and blinked hard at Rhonda.

"A moment of weakness. Stupidity, really. That's all I got to say about it."

The silence in the room settled. The only sounds came from the clacking of keys by the court reporter on the stenotype as she squinted with intensity, proofreading her work.

"The court appreciates the honesty," the judge said, smacking his lips and looking over some papers. "Ms. Pendleton," the

judge pronounced with earnestness in his voice, "this court sentences you to two years of prison, to be served at the Lakin Correctional Center and Jail in Point Pleasant."

Ken threw his hands over his head. "Judge, I object!"

"Mr. Fillmore—"

"Lakin is a maximum-security prison. My client violated her probation for selling drugs, not committing a murder—"

"Mr. Fillmore—"

"Lakin doesn't have the medical facilities to treat Hepatitis C. My client needs to be in a facility where she can get antibiotics and be monitored appropriately—"

The judge became incredulous. He slammed his gavel against the sound block. "Sit down, Mr. Fillmore."

"Your Honor," Ken pleaded, drawing out the last syllable for dramatic effect.

The judge slammed his gavel again. "Sit down, Mr. Fillmore. That is my last warning. Another outburst and I will find you in contempt of court."

The judge collected himself. "Our regional jails are overcrowded all over the state, and the individual counties don't have the money to pay for more inmates. I really have no choice. I can send your client to Lakin where they have space and where she can receive treatment,"

Rhonda slowly opened her eyes, and a cold chill coursed through her body. She rested her head in her hand and cast a glance at the narrow-barred window in the visitation room. Outside, the blue sky and mountain behind the prison lurched absurdly into the sky.

A voice called out from in front of her. "And then what?"

Rhonda looked up. The thin, angular face of her lawyer tightened, and her spindly neck and fingers flexed with tension. "My lawyer got removed from the courtroom because he didn't shut up. I was hauled out of court and brought here. I've been in this freakin' place ever since."

Lisa Escue nodded thoughtfully and made a note on her yellow legal pad, one of the few bright areas of color inside the dank, gray visitor room.

Lisa leaned over the table, and its fifteen-inch surface area was swallowed up under the notepad, pen, and leather folder. Rhonda hated meeting her here, but there was little choice. Prison was not a democracy, and Rhonda had learned quickly there were rules—lots of them. One being that Rhonda couldn't leave her seat at any time during the meeting. Rhonda and Lisa had been assigned seat three by one of the guards, which was located in the middle of the narrow room.

Rhonda strained to hear Lisa. With guards walking around, listening and watching, and the muffled conversations that other prisoners were having with their guests, the room was quite noisy.

The room was filled with every emotion imaginable—joy, tears, shame, anger, and everything in between. Rhonda had to block out the noise and the emotions and concentrate fully on what Lisa had to say. The conversation was important and would hopefully lead to Rhonda's release.

"I don't understand why I wasn't sent to the regional jail in Charleston," Rhonda whined, sounding more pitiful than forceful.

"There's a simple reason for that," Lisa answered, scribbling another sentence on her notepad. "The regional jails in Charleston and Barboursville are overcrowded and they don't have room for you. If you are juvenile, pregnant, have a mental illness, or are sick, they don't want you. It gives judges little options at sentencing."

Lisa peered up at Rhonda, her eyebrows so thick and animated they seemed ready to leap off of her forehead. Her blue eyes were bright and accentuated her ruddy complexion.

"And the Hep C?"

"I still got it," Rhonda answered, the words coming out in a harsh sputter. "I've been here two hundred and eighty-nine days. Two hundred and eighty-nine days! Away from my family, and you." Rhonda flopped back in her chair and folded her arms. "I'm eating lunch and taking showers with killers, Lisa. People who have killed other people. That ain't me. That ain't me at all."

She eyed Lisa intently then looked up and saw a guard pacing around the visitor's room, leering at them with a suspicious stare. In the two-way mirror at the end of the room, Rhonda scoffed at her complexion. She hated that she resembled an overgrown schoolgirl. Rosie-cheeked with wavy black hair, sparkling green eyes, and full lips, her vivid face always flushed and lit up with the emotions and ideas she was experiencing. Sometimes, Rhonda felt like Lisa talked to her like a child, and she wondered if her appearance had something to do with it.

Lisa sucked in a breath and exhaled it just as quickly. "Yes. I understand that you've been kept in solitary confinement while you've been here."

to pray, I heard something heavy collapsing behind me. I turned around and noticed a woman kneeling in front of a headstone two rows behind me. Intrigued and curious, my eyes narrowed on her. With a high forehead, brown hair, and oval-shaped glasses, the woman stared ahead with an expression both wary and challenging. Dressed in tan pants and boots and clad in a dark jacket, did not seem to fit in with the environment or the situation.

As the woman wept heavily, I noticed her rest an open hand on the surface of the headstone and watched as she dragged her fingers down the surface.

Then she fell back. I winced and waited for another sound. Instead, all I heard was a slight wind blowing through the cemetery. I stood up and took long strides toward her. As I got closer, I saw the woman stumble and pull herself upright. She reached inside a black knapsack and removed a bottle of whiskey. She fumbled with the lid at first, then ripped it off, tilted the bottle back, and chugged the contents.

"How much of that are you going to have?" I asked, slightly concerned and puzzled.

The woman stared ahead. "I'll let you know."

"When?"

"When I can't taste it anymore."

She tipped the bottle back again, taking three more large gulps. The whiskey trickled down her chin.

I folded my arms as she put the cap back on the bottle and tossed it aside.

"It appears you enjoy coming here as much as I do," I said, looking for a way into the conversation.

She sniffed and raked her hand across her wet chin. "I shouldn't even come here at all. That jerk doesn't deserve it."

I looked around the cemetery to see if anyone else was close by. Perhaps someone could help this woman. I did not have the internal fortitude today to handle it, but maybe someone else would. Across the grounds, nearly forty yards away, I noticed a small, dark speck move, but I assumed it was the sun playing tricks on my eyes. The woman rested her weight on two knees, and for the first time, looked up and locked eyes with me.

"Is there someone you love buried here?"

"Nope. We burned him."

I scrunched my face at the bluntness of her statement.

"Cremated him. Took some of his ashes down to Florida and scattered them over the Everglades. That was his favorite place, so we figured that was where he would want to be. We put the rest of him here." She dropped her head and pointed to the ground.

"My father is buried here." I began, but she cut me off.

"He was a lowlife, too. A stupid drunk who couldn't keep a job or keep his hands off Mama and me."

I jammed my hands into my pockets. "I'm sorry."

"I don't even know why I come here. It's not like we were close or anything. He always called me Daddy's girl, and he would coo at me like I was his pet. That was when Daddy was good before he drank. Then he'd leave and be gone for days on end, and when he came back, he was loaded and started swinging at Mama and me." The woman's voice quivered, and she dropped her head as tears streamed down her cheeks.

I looked over her shoulder and saw the same black speck shifting across the cemetery, although this time, the spot appeared larger and closer.

I dropped to one knee. Even though I knew nothing about this woman, I felt a strong connection to her because I sympathized with her feelings. My dad may not have been physically violent, but at times he was emotionally empty toward my mom and me. I wanted to say something that would comfort her, so I thought about what Dad always said about cemeteries.

"My father is buried right over there," I said, pointing ahead.

The woman's eyes slowly looked up, and she followed the direction of my finger.

"My dad spent a lot of time in cemeteries. Even though I hate coming here, I feel like being here puts me closer to him."

The woman nodded and then spoke. "I come here every week and talk to him. I'm not sure why, but I do. Heck, it's nearly cost me my job twice because I've missed work to come here. I feel guilty because Mama's too old and out of her mind to come and support me. I guess I do it for her and for me." She began to shriek in a high-pitched warble that made me step back. "For some reason, she always loved him no matter what." She lowered her voice. "It's ironic, you know. You can feel close to someone when being here, and at the same time, be assured that the person can never talk to you or touch you again. Sometimes, I want to be close to Daddy. Other times, I want to come here and let him know that he can never put his

hands on me again!" She extended her hand. "Help a lady up, will ya?"

I reached down and lifted her up. The woman weighed so little that I felt like I might catapult her over the fence.

"Thanks."

I turned around and saw her ruddy eyes and tear-stained cheeks. The wind tossed her hair over her shoulder. The ascending sunlight spread across her face, creating a large shadow that hid parts of her frail physique.

The woman turned and walked away without another word passing between us.

I returned to my dad's grave, completely forgetting the real reason I was there. However, someone else occupied the vacated space in front of the headstone—a man stood there, swiveling back and forth. My advance didn't startle him. In fact, he steadied himself after several moments of listless movement and then stopped moving all together.

I approached cautiously. From behind, the man had an elongated frame with a narrow waist. He wore a faded denim baseball cap pulled tightly over his head, only revealing the bottom lobes of his ears. Thick tufts of salt and pepper hair jutted out from under the base of the hat, and the scraggly arrangement of the hair made his entire head seem larger than the rest of his body. The man was familiar.

As I stepped closer, the man noticed me coming. I heard him inhale and then exhale a long, deep breath.

"I'll be out of your way in a minute." The man went back to swaying back and forth as he rummaged through a bag of tools, cleaners, and rags.